The Boys' Life Book of Horse Stories

For several generations, millions of boys all over America have been reading *BOYS' LIFE* magazine, the official publication of the Boy Scouts of America. Now *BOYS' LIFE LIBRARY* presents, in permanent form for all boys to enjoy, a rip-roaring roundup of ten of the most popular stories and articles about horses which have appeared in the magazine.

HAPPY BIRTHDAY   9th BIRTHDAY
JULY 9, 1965

FROM:
AUNT BEVE
UNCLE BARRY
COUSINS JILL
AND DICKIE

TO:
STEVE

The Boys' Life Book of Horse Stories

Selected by the Editors of *Boys' Life*

Illustrations by Sam Savitt

Random House   *New York*

Acknowledgments

The publishers wish to thank the following for permission to use these stories, all of which have appeared in *Boys' Life* magazine, copyright 1944, 1951, 1953, 1955, 1956, 1957, 1958, 1959, 1962, by Boy Scouts of America: Kerry Wood for WILD BRONC, B. J. Chute for TALE OF TWO HORSES, Stephen Payne for THE BLACK OUTLAW, Glenn Balch for WILD HORSE ROUNDUP, D. S. Halacy, Jr. for RIDE THE ROUGH STRING, Carl Henry Rathjen for THE CURB BIT, Vera E. Cline for THE MUDHEN, V.S., by Merritt P. Allen, Blanche Gregory for HORSE WITH COW SAVVY, by Joseph Stocker, Carl Henry Rathjen for SACRIFICE SPURS, Stephen Payne for BOSS OF THE CROSS-O.

Library of Congress catalog card number: 63-7837

Contents

Wild Bronc *by Kerry Wood*
3

Tale of Two Horses *by B. J. Chute*
23

The Black Outlaw *by Stephen Payne*
40

Wild Horse Roundup *by Glenn Balch*
62

Ride the Rough String *by D. S. Halacy, Jr.*
75

The Curb Bit *by Carl Henry Rathjen*
90

The Mudhen, V.S. *by Merritt P. Allen*
110

Horse with Cow Savvy *by Joseph Stocker*
126

Sacrifice Spurs *by Carl Henry Rathjen*
141

Boss of the Cross-O *by Stephen Payne*
164

The Boys' Life Book of
Horse Stories

Kerry Wood

Wild Bronc

Randy eased himself down from the top logs, carefully forking the saddle on Tame Jane. The raw-boned mare arched her back when she felt his weight, shrilling out a high squeal of rage as she fought against the rider. Her dark eyes rolled back, following the flattened line of her ears. She was a rough built brute, but there was power in every line. And Tame Jane did not want to be ridden. To show how she felt about it, she tried to kick her way out of the narrow chute. Randy Ganns had to jerk himself back onto the safety rail, to prevent having a leg mashed against the stout log sides.

"You ready, kid?" Pete asked, from the release gate.

"Not any more," Randy answered from his perch. He jockeyed for a good position again, ready to climb down when she stopped fighting. "Steady, girl—this won't hurt."

"Leastways," muttered Windy Smith. "It ain't likely to hurt her as much as it does you. Good luck, Randy."

"Yeah. Steady, now!" He settled into the saddle while Windy kept Tame Jane distracted. "Okay, Pete!"

The gate swung fast, then the mare took a plunging jump into the open corral. At once, Randy felt the surge of power in that tough big body. The jolt of her landing on bunched hooves shook the boy's spine, and before he could brace himself for the next shock, Tame Jane reared high. Her mane whipped across his face as he desperately leaned into the buck. Then her hind legs went up and her two front hooves came down with a crash. Randy pitched forward, the jack-knife action so fast that he hadn't time to catch his balance between the up and down rock. Before he could get a firm seat again, the squealing mare swapped ends and put down her head, trying to kick a hole in the sky. The young cowboy felt himself sailing through space.

Randy sprawled on the trampled dust and hurriedly rolled over, away from the active hooves of the angry mare. He had no desire to land back in the hospital he had left only recently. She didn't

bother him, however, but galloped away to the far side of the log corral to stand there quietly enough, though her intelligent eyes glowered at the watchers. The boy climbed painfully to his feet, dusting his jeans and picking up his battered hat.

"You lasted four jumps, that time," Jim Byers said, by way of offering sympathy.

"That's only one jump better than the other three tries," Randy answered ruefully. "She isn't even beginning to tire, Boss. She's a wild one, right enough."

"She sure is," agreed Windy Smith, who was sporting a skinned nose and a black eye. "I can't even stick her past the chute gate, and Pete here's no better."

"I don't want no more o' that bronc," Pete Malone grumbled, still limping from his last crash. "If Randy can't ride her, she just can't be ridden."

"I go for that, too," nodded Windy. "Randy's our best rider, Boss, and you see the trouble he has with her. Them DD ranch boys who named her Tame Jane sure love a joke, huh?"

Jim Byers, owner of the Circle-Bar ranch, leaned his lanky frame over the top log of the corral and studied the lady bronc critically, then shook his head.

"The DD boys were fair about it—they warned me she'd piled every one of their riders. But she's got good lines, in spite of that big-boned rawness. I had a notion she'd make a mighty fine riding horse; that's why I bought her with the rest of the DD broncs."

"Well, she sure don't ride easy, Boss," smiled Randy, rubbing his backside. "But she's not a killer—there's no mean streak in her. Maybe we could tame her in time, but I sorta think she's the kind that doesn't tame. Anyways, I'd appreciate a breather before I tackle her again."

Byers nodded. "You and the boys don't need to try her again, Randy. There's too much risk of crippling one of you, the way she bucks. But from here, she looks like a pretty powerful piece of horse-flesh, so I'm minded to turn her loose with the wild band up in the hills. She'll give us some colts that'll inherit that same powerful build. In any case, we've broken enough riding ponies out of the rest of the DD herd for our present needs, so tomorrow you boys can haze her and the other broncs back to the hills."

Windy and Pete cheered, then started chasing Tame Jane into the saddle chute again to strip off the leather.

"What're you grinning about?" Byers asked

Randy, as they waited beside the chute to help.

"I'm just glad you're keeping her, Boss," answered the boy. "I like that lady bronc. She fights you all the way, but she fights clean. She'll make a good addition to the hill herd—and I bet she becomes the leader pronto."

Randy was right. The raw-boned mare soon established her leadership over the unbroken horses that ranged the foothills on the back part of the Circle-Bar ranch. The hill range had everything the wild band needed: a mountain stream for water, lots of good fodder, and shelter in the stream-side evergreens when storms got fierce. The horses that roamed that hilly wasteland were always more than half wild, because Jim Byers and his cowboys didn't need to tend them much except during colt branding time and when they wanted to cut out a few extra horses for riding or for sale. The herd had been drastically thinned out during the last winter, however, when the blizzards had been the worst in years. That's why Byers was buying horses this spring instead of selling; he needed spare riding stock for his punchers and wanted to build up the hill herd to size again.

So Tame Jane became the leader of the wild band, and Randy Ganns was pleased to see the raw-boned, powerful animal galloping at the head of the herd. But the lady bronc had only been there in the hills a scant month when Mr. Haskell came calling at the Circle-Bar ranch house. D. J. Haskell was head of the Rodeo Stock Association that supplied most of the bucking horses for the rodeo and stampede shows of the west.

"I hear you got a wild bronc," Haskell said, pushing back from the chow table after eating with Byers and his cowboy gang. "The DD ranch boys tipped me off about Tame Jane. Said she'd piled six riders in a row. Before that, she was owned by the Bighorn Ranch and she broke a man's leg there. None of their waddies could sit her for more than two jumps."

"Randy lasted four," bragged Windy Smith. "Me, I'm strictly a one jump man."

"She spilled all of us," Pete Malone said.

Randy kept silent, anxiously watching Jim Byers. The boss was half-smiling at this banter, then became serious when he glanced across at the youngster who had joined his outfit so recently. He'd picked up Randy Ganns at a rodeo, where the boy had been trying to make a comeback after he had been injured and hospitalized. But the rancher had convinced him that he was better off as a workaday cowboy, so Randy had

turned his back on the stampede stuff. Jim Byers
liked the clean-cut youngster who was such a fine
rider. But he didn't know the boy very well as yet,
and Byers was a man who liked to know his riders.

"What about it?" Haskell demanded, unaware
of the cross-table tension growing between Byers
and Randy. "You've still got Tame Jane, haven't
you?"

"We've got her," Byers answered. "She's out
in the hills, leading our wild herd. And she's the
wildest of the lot."

"That's for me," beamed D. J. Haskell. "I've
checked her story at the DD and the Bighorn
ranches, and she sounds like a wonderful rodeo
horse. The wilder the better, because that's the
kind the crowds love to cheer. Tame Jane may
turn into the best rodeo bronc on my string, so I'll
pay top money for her."

Jim Byers was studying Randy Ganns closely,
sensing that the boy wanted him to keep the
horse. But the shrewd rancher had another idea;
here was his chance to learn what sort of stuff was
in this wandering rodeo cowboy he'd hired. He
suddenly smiled across the table at the tense
youngster and quietly said:

"Before you say anything about prices, Haskell,
I should mention that I gave Windy Smith and
Pete Malone a couple o' wild mares up there in

the hills. It gives 'em a little extra stake in the ranch, on top of wages. I haven't given you one as yet, Randy, because you've only worked for me a short spell. But to make everything fair and square, I think it's time you were cut in on the extras, too. And since you're so keen on that Tame Jane mare, I'm giving her to you here and now. Mr. Haskell, if you want to deal for that bronc, talk to her new owner."

The rodeo stock promoter turned and appraised the happy cowboy sitting beside him.

"She's not for sale," Randy told him, after thanking his boss for the gift.

"Everything's got a price," said D. J. Haskell. "Besides, when I talk about top money, I mean it. Of course, you got to realize that horse-flesh isn't in big demand anymore, what with every farmer owning a tractor nowadays."

"Yeah, but you can't herd cows with a tractor," Randy answered.

"Still, even here in the ranch country, you can buy your pick of trained saddle ponies for fifty to seventy-five dollars. Right? And I know for a fact that Jim Byers here paid the DD ranch only twenty dollars apiece for those unbroken broncs you've been working over, including Tame Jane. Before that, the Bighorn Ranch charged the DD boys fifteen dollars for her. So we've got a fair idea as to how much she's worth as a raw horse, on the regular market. But for my rodeo string, my top price for a good bucking bronc is two hundred dollars, cash!"

"Two hundred dollars!"

Jim Byers and his cowboys stared at Haskell. The offer was more than generous. And the Circle-Bar owner knew that Randy Ganns badly needed the money, because of the long stay in the hospital recovering from the rodeo injury. Randy still owed hospital and doctor bills.

"Take it!" urged Pete Malone.

"Grab it!" yelled Windy Smith.

Randy looked indecisive and confused. He'd been angry a moment ago, when Tame Jane was Circle-Bar property and he thought that Jim Byers was going to sell her for a rodeo bronc. But now she was his horse. And if he accepted the money, he could clear all his debts.

"Well—"

"Make up your mind, son," Haskell pressed. "That's my top price, so no haggling, please. Either take it or leave it."

"Gee!" Randy sounded miserable. "I'd sure love to leave it, Mister, but I owe some bills that've been fretting me terrible."

Haskell rose briskly to his feet, beaming his pleasure.

"I'll pay the moment she's loaded in my horse-trailer. It's hooked on behind my car, right now. I'll leave it down at your corrals, and you can load her from that saddling chute in the breaking corral. How long will you need to catch her?"

"That'll depend on the Boss, sir. I'll have to get her in my spare time, and it'll take some work to run her down."

But Jim Byers, smiling in a strange way, said: "No, Randy. We'll go after her right away, and I'll give you a hand myself. We can ride out to the hills this afternoon and scout the location of the herd, then camp out overnight and stalk her when she leads the herd to water at dawn. If we can get two lassoes on her, she'll handle easy enough. Take a stout halter, then we'll double lead her between our horses."

"Yeah," mumbled Randy. "Thanks a lot, Boss."

The owner of the Circle-Bar knew his range, so he guided Randy to the richest grass region of the hill country. That's where they sighted the wild horses, just as the sun was swinging low towards the purple-shadowed Rockies. The broncs made a wonderful picture, with sloping foothills rising steeply around three sides of their valley pasture and tall dark spruces on the far side. Some of the animals were sleek bays and chestnuts, a few were buckskins, blacks, and roans, while there were even a couple of dappled pintos to add variety to the band. And as watchful guardian over the feeding herd stood the raw-boned mare, Tame Jane.

"She's uneasy," Randy noted. "D'you think she senses us watching?"

"Probably," nodded Byers. "Some horses are like that. But we can outsmart her, this time. See: the valley is hemmed in with steep hills and cliffs, except for that spruce forest on the river side. This time o' year they'll avoid the spruces, because the flies aren't bad yet and out in these wilds, thick cover like that may hide a bear or a cougar. The way I dope it, Tame Jane will lead the band to water through that little ravine where the woods taper off and the hills start climbing. See it?"

"Yeah. And you figure we can post ourselves in the ravine?"

"There's a good trail leading down it, direct to the water. We can hide near that trail, and throw a loop on her as she comes along in the lead."

"But won't she smell us and our horses?"

"She'd sure smell our horses, or she'd hear 'em neigh. We won't take them into the ravine at all. But I think we can kill our own scent by rubbing

spruce needles over our clothing. It's worked before, for me."

"Sounds okay," Randy agreed. "What about
roping, though? We couldn't hold her, without
our horses to help."

"Sure we can. We'll pick a hide near a stout
tree, and snub onto that tree until we can fetch up
our saddle nags. Then we'll hem her in and snub
her tight, fastening on the halter and the double
lead-ropes. We shouldn't have any trouble this
time: she's in a sort of natural trap, right now."

"Yeah," muttered Randy, and he sounded dis-
appointed.

They ducked back on the screening side of the
ridge, riding down to the neck of the valley to
choose a hide just where the ravine opened onto
the river flats. A few scrub spruce provided a
natural blind, less than a dozen paces from the
narrow trail. There was a tough old stump nearby
on which to snub their ropes when they got a loop
around the mare's neck.

"It's made to order," Jim Byers said. "Just
about dawn, they'll come along here. They'll be
careless, being so close to water and wanting a
drink. And at this range, our throws can't miss."

Randy nodded, then followed the Boss back to
their horses. They made camp a quarter mile
down stream, against a cliff that shielded their fire.

Randy collected willow wood and built up a bed of coals, then put on a bannock to bake and fried some sow-belly. A pot of rice and raisins simmered on a jigger-stick, for dessert.

"Good cooking," commented the Boss, after the meal. "Where'd you learn that stuff?"

"While following the rodeos," Randy answered. "I never won much prize money, so I had to live kinda careful between shows. I'd ride my Banjo horse from show to show, camping along the trail. Buying the makin's for camp meals was a lot cheaper than paying for restaurant chow."

Byers asked: "How did you like the rodeo life, kid?"

"Oh, it had its ups and down. I got good horses to ride, but I'm a workaday rider, like you once said. I didn't know how to make my rides look showy. So others got top money while I collected bruises."

"It was a beef that sent you to hospital, wasn't it?"

"Yeah. One o' them tough Brahma bulls. After it threw me, it rammed me. Smashed a few ribs and battered me up a bit. I was in hospital a whole month."

"That's why you need Haskell's two hundred, eh?"

"Yeah. I wanna be clear of debt, but—"

"But what?"

Randy reached forward to add more fuel to the campfire, and the Circle-Bar owner noted Randy's tight frown as the orange flames leaped up and lighted his face.

"Well, I was just thinking about Tame Jane, fenced in there at the rodeo corrals," Randy said, after a moment. "I guess it isn't too hard on a horse, being forked by riders a couple times a day and putting on a bucking show for a few minutes, but—"

He lapsed into silence.

"She'll be well fed and cared for," Jim Byers said. "Haskell treats his stock good, no question of that."

"Oh, I know. But there's the ballyhoo of rodeos. Calliope music, sideshow juke boxes, brass bands in front of the grandstands. My Banjo horse could never get used to it, nor the shouts of barkers, and the loud-speakers yelling out who's coming out on Number Two Chute—Randy Ganns on Widow-maker, or something like that. Then the roaring cheer of the grandstand crowd, with flags waving, cars honking, and everything noisy all the time. It kinda bothered me, until I was actually on a bronc and too busy riding to notice."

"Maybe the bronc is too busy to notice, too."

"Yeah, well— I mean, while you're just hanging around, it's a sort of phony life. Crowds and more crowds, noise all the time, and always on the jump from show to show." He stood up, pointing. "See that ole yellow moon, climbing over the hills? Hear that yodeling coyote, and the hoot-owl, and the sing-song of the river? That's for me, Boss; this is what I like."

"Me, too, fella." Jim Byers agreed, smiling.

They didn't talk any more, bedding down to get an early start before dawn.

They were hidden in the scrub spruce by the time the first green light of morning snuffed out the stars. Both had rubbed evergreen needles over hands and clothing, the pungent smell of the spruce neutralizing the human scent. Byers noted that the dawn breeze was favorable, blowing from the trail directly towards them. They had their lariats all ready, looped and coiled for quick throwing.

"We can't miss," the Boss said.

"Guess not," agreed Randy.

He caught a whiff of sage smell above the sharper scent of the spruce needles they'd crushed. Randy watched the blue shadows of the hills, looming large against the brightening eastern sky. As the light became stronger, the shadows changed from blue to grey, then he made out details of rocks and trees and shrubs. A small creature moved along the sky-line: it was a long-eared jack rabbit, seeking a day bed. Byers touched his shoulder, pointing. Randy turned to see a doe and her spotted fawn, wading into the shallows of the river to nuzzle the water for their morning drink. When a coyote's yapping howl rose not far away, the nervous doe quickly led her fawn into the screening shelter of bank willows.

"Won't be long now," whispered the Circle-Bar rancher.

"Yeah," muttered Randy.

He strained to listen for the distant thud of hooves that would announce the coming of the wild band. He heard the tuk-tuk-tuka of a sharp-tailed grouse, poised on a poplar top. A vesper-bird was whistling from a nearby rock, a cheery little song that was pleasant to hear. And over in the spruce forest a hermit thrush was fluting—the finest bird music he knew.

"You hear 'em?" asked Byers.

"I hear 'em," answered Randy. "Oh—you mean the horses? No; not yet."

Then, suddenly, he did hear them. A drubbing noise, faint at first but soon growing loud. Tame Jane was bringing them fast, at full gallop down the narrow trail. He heard a trumpeting neigh from the herd stallion, answered by the softer whickering of a mare. Then the thudding became a thunder as the herd raced down the draw.

"Ah, look at 'em!" breathed Randy.

Tame Jane was at the head, pounding along at an easy lope. Her head was proudly high, her tail flowing out as her long legs arched over the ground. Behind her, the band of wild ones came in single file, their heads stretched forward and the first rays of the morning sun glinting on their colors, the brown and blacks, the tan buckskins and white-blotched pintos.

"Get set!" whispered Byers.

But Randy put a hand on the Boss' throwing arm, holding him still.

"Quick, now," whispered Byers. "She'll be opposite, in a sec."

"Wait!" urged Randy, watching every move of the powerful mare. "She's something of a beauty, Boss, in her own big-boned way."

"Yep. Got your rope?"

"No," said Randy, and his fingers dug into the older man's arm to hold him down. "Look at them run! Gee—don't they look swell?"

"Hey—we're too late!"

"Never mind," the young cowboy said. "I'm not gonna turn that wild beauty into a rodeo bucking outlaw. Haskell can keep his two hundred—let 'er go!''

They watched in silence while the broncs went to water, thrusting thirsty muzzles into the crystal mountain waters. Then Tame Jane's head came up, whirling around to stare at the scrub spruce alongside the ravine path. A whistling snort came from her, whereupon the whole band raised their heads, alert to her warning. Next moment the leader turned and plunged into the deep water, churning across the river with the herd at her heels.

"Ya-hoooooo!" cheered Randy.

Tame Jane put speed into her strides and the horses squealed their alarm as they charged up the far bank.

"Yiiiiiiiiiiiiiiii!" shrilled Jim Byers, waving his big hat.

The herd thundered across the flats, then Tame Jane led them up a hillside. For a moment more the galloping broncs were in view, charging up the slope. Tame Jane stopped on the crest, the morning sun behind her. She looked back at the men, shrilling her defiance. Next instant she whirled away, leading the wild band over the ridge and out of sight.

Jim Byers replaced his hat, grinning at Randy.

"So! You're not selling the lady bronc, eh?"

"No, sir. Let her live out here where it's wild and pretty. It's what she likes, and that's what I'd like for her as long as I own her."

"What about your debts?"

"I been thinkin' about them, too. Windy Smith offered me seventy-five dollars for my fancy rodeo saddle, and Pete wants to buy my tooled bridle, cuffs, and spurs for another twenty-five. There's a hundred bucks I can raise, right away."

"I'll advance you the other hundred, against your wages," suggested Byers. "Looks like you'll be staying on the Circle-Bar for a spell, so it's okay to give you any advance you want."

"I'll be staying, Boss," smiled Randy. "Me and Tame Jane over there—we like it here!"

The boy wondered why the rancher shook hands right then, but Jim Byers had his reasons. He liked knowing his men, and the Circle-Bar boss liked what he knew about young Randy.

B. J. Chute

Tale of
Two Horses

Buzz Thompson shot
into the living room, seized upon his brother, who
was peacefully settled in an armchair, and waved
a letter under his nose.

Jim sighed a resigned sigh and unwound from
the cushions. "It's from Tommy," he deduced,
peering at the envelope. "I recognize what he
laughingly calls his handwriting."

"Big news," said Buzz. "He wants us to spend
next month with him in the country, and his
father is buying a horse."

"A what?"

"A horse."

"Why?" said Jim reasonably.

Buzz looked at his brother with genuine pain.
"You do manage to ask the darnedest questions,"
he complained. "How should I know why? They
want to ride it, I suppose. Here, I'll read what he

says." He unfolded the letter and began to decipher it, picking his way carefully among the blots. " 'We want you and Jim to spend a month' —it looks like youth, but I guess it's month—'with us in the country. Dad has'—it looks more like bisected, but I guess it's decided—'Dad has decided to buy a horse, and we will have a sweee time—' "

"What kind of a time?"

"Sweee. S-w-e-e-e. New slang term, I guess." Buzz glared at the page and then gave a triumphant yelp. "Oh, I get it—it's 'swell.' 'We will have a swell time. So let me know if you can come next wouth—month—and give my regards to everybody. Your pal, Tommy.' Whoosh!" He heaved exhaustedly and collapsed on the sofa. "How's that for a swell invitation?"

"Sweee, you mean," said Jim. "Very sweee indeed. A horse, huh? They must be renting that same place on the Bay they had last summer."

"Probably." Buzz became suddenly pensive. "Jim, I've been thinking—"

"It's the company you keep," said Jim unsympathetically. "You can't say I haven't warned you."

"Hush your fuss. I've been thinking about Tommy and the horse. Do you remember the

Christmas vacation we spent with him and his father at that cabin?"

Jim shuddered delicately. "I do indeed. They put us on skis and then skied circles around us, while we fell into every snowdrift in sight. I was a fine old Roman ruin, I was. Why? What put skis in our head?"

"The horse. It's just occurred to me," said Buzz in sepulchral tones, "that the horse is going to be exactly like the skis. By next month, Tommy is going to know all about riding, while we—"

Jim said thoughtfully, "I see what you mean."

A deep silence settled over the room, during which Buzz sank lower and lower into the sofa, his feet waving in the air. Then he gave a sudden shout and surged upwards. "I've got it!"

Jim said mildly that he hoped it wasn't catching.

Buzz ignored him. "What we'll do," he said firmly, "is learn to ride before we go out there. Then—"

"Riding lessons," said Jim, "cost millions."

"True. But it doesn't cost much to rent a horse, especially if we aren't fussy, and we could teach ourselves in a week. I'll study it up first at the library, and in no time we'll be galloping in all directions. Then we can give good old Tommy the shock of his career, and besides we'll enjoy our month in the country ten times as much.''

"Okay," said Jim, having spent most of his life being resigned to his brother's ideas.

One of the hired horses was named Clementine, and the other Lightning, which struck Jim as a peculiar combination. Buzz said airily that names didn't mean anything, and then seized Clementine's reins and said he would ride her. Jim said, didn't he think he would prefer Lightning? Buzz said, no, no, he wanted Jim to have only the best and a horse named Lightning must be good.

"He'd better be," said Jim grimly, stroking Lightning's ears and murmuring "Nice horsie" with some doubt.

"I shall now," said his brother learnedly, "impart to you the information I collected from the library. The initial step is mounting."

Jim said it seemed logical.

"First," said Buzz, suiting the action to the word, "we put our left foot in the stirrup. Oh, help! I'm splitting!" He grabbed for the saddle and hung on desperately, remarking over his shoulder that no horse should be allowed to grow so tall. "You do the same thing with Lightning, Jim."

Jim sighed, took hold of the saddle and swung

one leg up to the stirrup. He miscalculated his distances, gave Lightning an involuntary kick in the ribs and came back to earth. Lightning, with considerable restraint, merely turned his craggy head and gave his would-be rider a hard look.

"Well, I'm *sorry*," Jim muttered. He then added that if he had known he was going mountain climbing he would have brought a rope and a St. Bernard dog.

"Swing the leg up easily," said Buzz.

"Unquote," said Jim bitterly, sighed, swung the leg up and, to everyone's surprise, got his foot into the stirrup.

"Good," his brother approved. "Now, we bound into the saddle."

"Bound?" said Jim in a quiet voice.

"Bound," said Buzz. "Like this." He bounded upwards, throwing his right leg about in a graceful manner. As a bound it was splendid, and it had the added attraction of getting him well into the air above Clementine. Unfortunately, he bounded too far, started to go off the other side, and only saved himself by a last second grab at the reins.

Clementine gave a snort. So did Jim.

"Seems to me you bounded right out of bounds," said Jim critically. "*I* shall simply climb. Hold still, Lightning old boy. I'm a-comin'."

No one could have called it a spirited ascent,

and it was accompanied by considerable impassioned grunting, but time brings all things and eventually the heights of Lightning were scaled and Jim was in the saddle.

"You don't happen to have an oxygen mask handy, Buzz?" he inquired. "Air's rather thin up here. What on earth are all these reins for?"

"Snaffle and curb," Buzz supplied promptly with an air of vast learning, and dug in his pocket for a piece of paper. "I had to write down about how to hold them, because it's rather complicated. Let's see—left snaffle outside little finger of left hand, left curb between third and fourth fingers, right snaffle between thumb and forefinger—whoops!—curb rein between first and second and—"

After a moment, Jim said politely, "What's it going to be when you've finished knitting it?"

Buzz looked down at his inextricably wound-up fingers and said candidly that he really didn't know yet but he thought it might make a nice tea cozy. "Look, pal, *you* read the instructions to me, huh? Here."

It took ten minutes' hard work to organize the reins, and Clementine became thoroughly bored and took to shifting her feet around and making outraged snuffling noises.

"Okay," said Buzz at last. "Here we go. Come

on, Clemmy. Allez-oop." He then stuck his heel into her side, and Clementine did the allez while Buzz did the oop. Another frenzied grab at the reins corrected her impression that he desired speed, but the look she gave him would have withered a less sensitive soul than Buzz's.

"We'll just walk at first," said Buzz. "Quietly and with dignity."

Quietly and with dignity, they walked. A beautiful calm settled on them all. It was a lovely day, and the view from the horses' backs was most pleasing. Buzz began to hum something to the effect that he was a lone cowhand and Jim joined in. A feeling of tremendous competence seized them, and Buzz interrupted a survey of his intentions toward the Rio Grande to observe that Tommy was going to turn bright purple with surprise when he saw them in action.

Jim nodded happily, lulled by the soothing rhythm. "And what does the book tell us to do next?"

"Trot," said Buzz. "All very simple. One merely shortens the reins—thus—touches the horse with the heel—thus—and—hey, Clementine! Wait!"

For Clementine, a cooperative little lady if ever there was one, had obediently begun to trot. She rose and Buzz rose with her, but it was the last time that happened. She caught him on the second bounce, and the next time she rose Buzz was coming down.

"Yoicks!" Buzz yelled. "Gurk! Clementine! WHOA!"

Clementine kept gaily on, leaving Lightning and Jim behind her in the road. Jim observing anxiously and trying to deduce from Buzz's exhibition just what the library had said about trotting, shook his head in a mystified manner. That close sympathy between horse and rider which is so invaluable seemed somehow to be lacking. Any contact established between Buzz and Clementine was purely coincidental.

"Well, well," said Jim, and absentmindedly gathered up the reins which he had allowed to slacken on Lightning's neck. Lightning, mistaking this for an invitation to the waltz and anxious to catch up with Clementine, who was a dear old pal of his, gave a heave like a depth charge, collected himself, and burst into a fine free canter.

The first heave sent Jim up out of the saddle and when he came down he was practically sitting on Lightning's tail. The next heave corrected this situation, and Jim moved up front with his nose buried in the horse's mane and his arms wound

passionately around its neck. Lightning caught up with Clementine in two leaps.

"Help!" yelled Buzz, under the fond impression that he was being rescued.

"Help! Help!" yelled Jim, losing his right stirrup and all hope in the same moment. "Lightning, whoa! Halt! Hold still! Horse, be reasonable!"

Lightning, faintly disconcerted by a rider who evidently thought he was a necklace, slowed down, gave a few unpleasant bounces, and then came to a puzzled halt. Jim grunted piteously, unwound his arms from their stranglehold and slid gently to earth.

Clementine stopped trotting so suddenly that Buzz nearly went off over her head.

"Oooooo-woooh!" said Buzz.

Jim lay on the ground for a moment, then rolled over and got to his hands and knees. He then gave a stricken yelp, announced that he was done for forever, and presented Lightning with what could only be described as a dirty look. Lightning, however, was thoughtfully chewing a piece of landscape at the moment and missed it.

"I'm ruined," said Jim.

Buzz said, "I think you were cantering. *I* was trotting." He then added, "At least, Clementine was trotting. I was working against her. Jim—"

"Yes?" said Jim in hollow tones, arising stiffly.

"It seems to me," said his brother, "that we should walk home very quietly. How does it seem to you?"

"To me," said Jim, "it seems that we should be carried home on a stretcher. Two stretchers. Buzz, this was *your* idea."

Buzz admitted that it was. He then had a typical resurgence of optimism, entirely owing to the fact that Clementine was standing still. "Our great mistake was in not learning what to do with a trot and canter. There must be methods—I just didn't read far enough. Tomorrow," he said, "we will do it right."

"Tomorrow?" his brother murmured faintly. "Look, you may be a relative, but there *are* limits. For me and Lightning, there is no tomorrow. We have quit."

"Tomorrow." Buzz was firm. "Think of spending that month with Tommy and having him gloating over us. Besides," he added devastatingly, "I've paid for the horses in advance."

He then turned Clementine's head toward home by the simple means of pulling on a rein, and this success so excited him that he was quite bright and cheerful until he got to the stables and slid to earth, whereupon he began groaning again, very symphonically.

But he groaned even more the next morning when he woke up.

Jim, wakened by these sad sounds, rolled over lightheartedly in bed and immediately regretted the rash act. Jointly the brothers sat up and howled.

"It will wear off," said Buzz after a moment of feeling his bones. "The best cure for stiffness is doing the same thing over again. Now, about trotting, it seems that my mistake was in not posting. One should rise to the trot. It's all a matter of rhythm, and today I fully expect to master it. As to the canter—"

"I don't want to hear about it," said Jim between his teeth.

"Oh, yes, you do," Buzz assured him. "What you should do in the canter is sit back and relax."

"Ha."

"Keeping," said Buzz, "the spine erect."

"Ha, ha. Did you say erect or wrecked?"

"You'll love it. By tonight, everything will be different."

This was, in a sense, quite true. Everything was different because they were both stiff in entirely new places. Buzz's merry optimism about posting turned out to be quite unfounded, and he and Clementine were still working counterclockwise with all decisions going to Clementine. Lightning,

on the other hand, simply didn't like to trot.
Lightning liked to canter.

The morning's outing, therefore, consisted of
Buzz going out-two-bump-three-bump, and Jim
going heave-bump-crash-heave. By the time it
was over, the only thing that kept Jim sticking
grimly to the proposition was the strictly com-
mercial point of view he had toward Buzz's cash
transaction with the stables.

The next day, however, he succeeded in getting
Lightning to trot. His impression that he had
plumbed the depths of equestrian experience was
thereby corrected. He had not, it seemed, even
skimmed the surface. Lightning's version of trotting was high, wide, and frightful, and he got a
gruesome tilt to his ears and a look in his eye that
made it perfectly plain to Jim that the whole
thing was a plot.

"Splendid," gasped Buzz, bouncing at his side.
Buzz was trying to get Clementine to canter, and
Clementine was compromising on a sort of sideways galumph that was first cousin to a train
wreck. "But you're—supposed—to—rise in the—
saddle."

"I *am* rising," Jim shrieked. "And I don't like
it!"

"On—purpose—I mean," said Buzz, coming

down suddenly where Clementine wasn't and grabbing for a handful of mane to re-establish their relationship. "Look, horse, darn you—canter!"

He lifted the reins recklessly and gave them a good hard shake. The inevitable immediately happened, and good little Clementine, full of goodwill, surged obediently upwards.

As a canter, it was beautiful but brief. Buzz automatically grabbed for more mane, clutched her tail instead on the way out, and ended sitting on the roadside in a patch of thistles.

This was the point at which Jim clearly should have dismounted and gone to his brother's aid. Unfortunately, this was instead the point at which Lightning suddenly bolted for home.

"That's a nice brotherly act for you," said Buzz bitterly, and, rising slowly from the ground, he began to remove some of the sharper thistles from his person.

When the brothers met again, Jim was reclining pitifully on a couch with six sofa pillows at strategic points. Buzz, limping into the room, decided he would lean on the mantelpiece for reasons best known to himself.

A weighty silence filled the room and then the doorbell rang twice.

"You go," said Jim, not stirring.

"Postman," said Buzz thinly.

"Oh."

More silence. Finally Jim said plaintively, "You're standing up already. It wouldn't kill you to stagger to the door."

"My staggering days are over," said Buzz.

"Oh," said Jim. Another silence. Then, "It might be a letter."

"I don't care if it's a rhinoceros coming by parcel post, I'm not going to move for anyone." He then added, "Darn you," very feelingly and crawled off to the door.

Jim readjusted a cushion and sighed.

Buzz came back with an envelope. "It's from Tommy," he said, slitting it and opening the letter out. "Dear Buzz," he read, "it was—uh'm —swell to hear you and Jim are coming—uh— something the weather something. Well, *something* about the weather, and then a blot. The horse—"

There was a sudden pause that stretched out unexpectedly.

Jim raised himself tenderly on one elbow. "Well?"

"The horse—the horse—" Buzz's voice sounded rather strained.

A slightly stricken look appeared on Jim's face. "Well, *read* it. What's happened to the horse?"

"The horse—" Buzz gulped, closed his eyes,

opened them again, and then read the next sentence very fast. "The horse has five bedrooms and a beautiful view."

Jim forgot that he was a broken man and sat upright on the couch. "WHAT?"

"You heard me," said Buzz, sounding pale. "The horse has five bedrooms and a beautiful view, Jim—" He gulped again. "Jim, I'm very much afraid we read Tommy's first letter wrong. I'm afraid his father has bought a house, not a horse."

"This," said Jim, "is the end." He laid himself back on the cushions.

"Yes," said Buzz.

"I hold you personally responsible for all my bones," said Jim. "It was you who misread that letter. It was you who insisted on hiring those two equine fiends. It was you who—"

"Yes," said Buzz.

There was some more silence. "And furthermore," said Jim severely, "henceforth I shall turn a deaf ear to all your bright ideas. Go away and have them somewhere else."

"Yes," said Buzz very meekly, and went back to lean on the mantelpiece. But after a moment he turned around and added, "But you know, Jim, I *did* get Clementine to canter. It seems a

pity to waste all we've learned, and really everyone ought to be able to ride a horse—"

"Buzz!" Jim started to rise from the couch,
then sank back with a howl of pain. "Listen, if
you're suggesting that I deliberately get on top of
one of those four-footed roller coasters again, all I
can say is you're stark staring mad."

"You'll learn to love it," said Buzz, unmoved.
He then added, "Besides, the horse is man's
noblest friend, and who are you to spoil a beautiful friendship?"

Jim gave a hoarse laugh. Under the circumstances there was nothing else for him to do.

Stephen Payne

The
Black Outlaw

Dale Harmon rode with his eyes on lofty mountains against the far western horizon. With luck, he'd cross Feather Edge Range tomorrow or next day and reach his uncle's big cattle ranch, where he'd have the fun and the hard work of riding a real roundup.

Dale's immediate problem however was to find a place to put up for the night. So, hoping to locate some not too distant camp, settler's shack, or ranch, the young cowboy urged tiring Buttons to the crest of a high, rocky, pinon-and-cedar-studded ridge which broke the monotony of sage brush hills.

Luck was with him, for in the narrow valley at his left he saw a small, fenced ranch and a spring-fed stream. At the foot of the ridge stood a rough lumber cabin and a shed, as well as a pole corral out of which a man was leading a beautiful coal black horse, saddled and bridled, stepping quietly.

Dale was about to urge Buttons down the slope when a gruff voice startled both horse and rider. "Hey, you! Keep away from down there!"

Dale turned his head and saw a tall lean fellow who stepped out from behind a huge rock. Dressed like a cowboy, the man had hawkish features, and his sharp gray eyes were definitely unfriendly and challenging.

"Why should I keep away?" Dale retorted, temper rising.

"Because," the man returned, craning his neck for a look into the valley, "I see you're a cowpuncher. So o' course you don't want anything to do with a dirty squatter!"

But Dale had heard the squeal of an infuriated horse, and again his gaze traveled to the spot below the ridge where the man had mounted the black, which was now bucking with terrific fury.

Dale's eyes grew bright. "Ride him, cowboy!" he yelled, and started Buttons down the incline.

At this, the tall fellow made a desperate attempt to grasp Buttons' bridle. The clever pony dodged, and then raced down the slope with the speed of an eagle swooping down.

Dale had acted none too quickly, for the black

tornado soon hurled the unfortunate rider into the dust. The next instant the horse charged, teeth bared viciously, front feet striking the fallen man.

Buttons had cleared a fence and rushed on, while Dale jerked his rope free of the strap at his saddle fork and built a loop in the honda end. This done, he crashed Buttons into the black, knocking it away from its victim. Dropping his loop around the horse's neck, Dale snubbed it to his saddle horn and half dragged it toward the corral, where he tied it to a post.

To the young cowboy's relief, the man was sitting up, dazed and staring, as if scarcely comprehending what had happened. A tall, thin fellow of about thirty-five, in bib overalls and heavy work shoes, he had lost his hat, and blood from a scalp wound was trickling down one whisker-stubbed cheek.

"Take it easy," said Dale practically, "while I find out if you're badly hurt." A minute later, "Your right hand's bruised. But no bones broken. What in thunderation were you trying to do?"

"Trying something I shouldn't have tried— taking horses to break."

" 'Horses to break?' " Dale repeated, and counted eleven horses in the corral. Two, a work

team, the others, range mustangs with long tails and long, ragged manes.

"Yes," the man said, getting to his feet. He gritted his teeth as he felt of his right shoulder and winced as he put his weight on his right leg. "I'm trying to hold down my homestead. But with no money and nothing to sell, I went to Jeff Strong of the Z-Bar-2 twelve miles south and asked for work. It's the nearest ranch, because this country is really nothing but sage desert, except for a few good springs, like in this valley I've taken up. But sheepmen graze flocks hereabouts in the winter, and Strong has both cattle and sheep."

"Did he give you a job breaking horses?"

The man recognized Dale's incredulity, and smiled somewhat ruefully. "Jeff Strong hadn't any ranch job, but he did have nine geldings he wanted broken to work, not to ride. Back home on the farm, I have broken horses to harness, so I took the job."

"Now I understand," said Dale, "for almost anybody can break a horse to work." He gave his name, and asked the settler's.

"Fred Gordon, and I hope you'll stay over night with me, Dale . . . something else puzzling you?"

"Yes. What about this black outlaw? I see it's

branded Z-Bar-2 like the others. Now it's quieted down it seems well-broken and gentle."

"I didn't have a saddle horse, so Strong offered me the use of this black because I must pasture the horses in my field and wrangle them every morning."

"Did he say it was gentle?" Dale asked, feeling a chilly suspicion that Strong might have supplied this horse, hoping it would kill the settler.

"Strong said the horse was safe even for a farmer like me," Gordon replied. "Today, one of his men delivered the horses, and I found the black easy to catch and gentle to saddle. Then— well, you saw what happened."

"Yes, I saw," said Dale, swinging up.

"Not going on, are you?" Gordon inquired anxiously.

"I'll be back," Dale promised, and rode to the top of the ridge to cut for sign. But he did not find the tall man, and the coming of darkness put an end to his search.

After his return to the homesteader's ranch, Dale decided not to alarm Fred Gordon, but he did ask for a description of Jeff Strong and of the rider who had delivered the horses. The description of the latter, Sid Brooks, tallied with that of the fellow Dale had seen.

For a long time Dale lay awake, troubled and

disturbed, facing the hardest decision of his life.

He had grown up on a prairie ranch where all of the country was fenced and much of it farmed. But beyond Feather Edge Range of mountains, in a land not yet fenced and settler-squeezed, thousands of cattle still grazed the wide-open range, and this fall Dale's Uncle, Clint Harmon, had sent word, "If your folks'll let you, Dale, get over here by September fifth for my beef round-up."

Dale was a good hand with stock, particularly horses. Yet until now he'd had no opportunity of working on a big outfit with real cowpunchers, and he did not want to miss that roundup.

Fred Gordon had however told Dale how much he wanted to make a home for his wife and their two children. If he earned the hundred dollars Jeff Strong had promised, provided the job was finished in two weeks—he could send for them. Yet now that he'd been hurt, it was impossible for him to break the horses.

"Aw, I won't get soft," muttered Dale, tossing restlessly. "I've no use for settlers, and I'd be crazy to get mixed up in a fight for range where I'll be siding a nester against a big rancher. Yet what if Sid Brooks and Jeff Strong try again to get Fred killed?"

Thinking of this sinister threat, Dale reluctantly

came to the decision that regardless of his own ambitions, he must help Gordon and see him through this crisis.

Accordingly, at daybreak he brought Buttons in off picket and wrangled all the other horses. When he looked again at the black outlaw, he realized that it was a magnificent animal, and he suddenly wanted to prove to himself that he could break the horse of his vicious habits, and really tame him.

Gordon was stiff and sore, and his right hand so nearly useless that he turned the pancakes with his left, yet he nevertheless cooked the breakfast. His despondency vanished, and his blue eyes lighted with reborn hope when Dale said off-handedly, "I reckon I can lay over a day or two and help you with those broncs, Fred. I'd also like to take the kinks out of that outlaw. 'Comet' will be a good name for him."

Having thus committed himself, Dale hurried to the corral, hoping work would make him forget the roundup he was missing. Catching one of Gordon's team, Dale cinched the settler's saddle on its back. He then roped and threw one of the green broncs, put a strong halter on its head and tied it to the saddle horn—an easy way to halter break a bronc, since the patient and sturdy work horse relieved a man of the hard work.

Next, Dale roped and saddled Comet. A moment later, he was making the supreme ride of his life on the savage bucker. By pulling leather, he managed to stay until Comet winded himself and stopped fighting.

All out of breath, Dale called to Gordon to open the gate and stand behind it, out of the horse's reach. He then rode Comet out into the field and gave him a hard workout. Returning to the corral, he coaxed the horse close to the fence, and dismounted on it. Comet reared and struck at him, but Dale was safe on the other side.

With Gordon helping as much as he could, the two halter-broke four more horses. That done, Dale knocked off early, rode up on the ridge to scout, and found both hoof prints and fresh boot marks. Someone had been spying on Gordon's ranch today! It gave Dale an apprehensive feeling. However, if Brooks was intending to dry gulch either Gordon or Dale, he'd surely have tried it by now.

In the long days that followed, Dale really enjoyed the hard work, although whenever he thought of the roundup he was missing he felt impatience and irritation. However, since he had counted on answering his uncle's letter in person, Uncle Clint would not worry. He'd decide, "Dale couldn't make it."

The urgency of getting all the broncs gentled prevented him from making a trip to Strong's ranch for a showdown. So many horses to handle, only two weeks to finish the job! Dale and Fred would hitch a green horse to the wagon with one of Gordon's gentle team and drive around the field, repeat this with another and another until they learned what was expected.

At noon of the tenth day, Dale told Gordon, whose cuts and bruises were improving fast, "We're going to win!" Then he frowned. "But I'm still uncertain about Comet."

Sometimes the black was as well-mannered as a horse could be, almost fooling Dale into a sense of security. Again, like a change of wind, he would become his earlier vicious, man-killing self. Twice his ripping teeth and flashing hoofs almost caught Dale, but the cowboy escaped by sheer agility.

Gordon straightened from looking into the oven where biscuits were baking. "Yes, thanks to you, cowboy, I'll make good with Jeff Strong. But I wish I had some steady way of making a living. If I could just get a band of sheep! Summers I could graze them near the ranch, and water them at the spring; then, during the winter, farther out in the hills, and—"

"With sheep, you'd soon be sitting pretty,"

Dale finished for him, though he couldn't really sympathize with such an ambition. "Any hope you might buy a flock?"

"None," replied Gordon. "Nor is there any hope I can hang on to my claim here."

Contrary to Dale's expectations, he had come to like the settler tremendously while batching and working with him. Dale simply had to admire Gordon's grit and his doggedness of purpose in trying to establish himself as a ranchman.

"The more I think about it," Gordon continued in a bitter tone, "the more certain I am that Jeff Strong hoped that black outlaw would kill me. Am I right, Dale?"

Dale nodded and spoke through tight lips. "A range hog sheepman would hate you and want to take this good valley away from you. I think the only reason someone hasn't tried again to kill you in some accidental appearing manner is because I'm here. But after I've gone—" He left the rest to Gordon's inference.

However, the two agreed to postpone the showdown with Strong until all of the horses were thoroughly broken. Early the following morning, they hooked a team of the broncs to the wagon, and drove out onto the open range to give them a thorough workout.

Upon their return to the ranch toward noon, Dale's eyes went at once to the corral where all the other horses were penned. "Fred!" he cried, "there's a black horse we've not seen before in that corral. But Comet isn't there!"

Gordon looked. "The black outlaw gone! Another horse left in its place! What can this mean?"

"It means," snapped Dale, "that Strong or Brooks, or both of them, have put over a fast and tricky play on us . . . I should have suspected this very thing."

"You're not to blame," Gordon said. "What can they expect to gain by switching horses?"

"You'll see," Dale rapped out furiously. "Let's head for the Z-Bar-2. Dog the luck. I wonder if somebody'll get Comet all worked up and crazy once again when I was just winning the outlaw's confidence."

Mastering the outlaw meant a great deal to Dale and at this critical stage he hated to have his good work undone by someone else.

The two were soon mounted, Dale on Buttons, Gordon on the strange black which proved to be a docile plug. When they arrived at the Z-Bar-2, Dale saw a man, who apparently had just driven in from another direction, unhitching a team from a buckboard.

"That's Jeff Strong," said Gordon.

Dale thought "Strong" a good name for the solidly built, weather-beaten ranchman. Well past middle age, he had iron gray hair and clipped gray mustache.

Prepared to hate and distrust the man, Dale nevertheless approved of the twinkle in the shrewd eyes, and the hearty greeting certainly sounded sincere.

"Why, hello, Gordon. Good to see you. How you making out with those broncs? Who's your friend?"

"He's Dale Harmon, a cowboy who came along just in time to stop that black outlaw you gave me for a saddle horse from killing me," Gordon replied.

"Black outlaw?" Strong exclaimed. "The horse you're riding is old Pete, the gentlest horse on the outfit. I told Sid Brooks to deliver him to you along with the other stock. Would have done it myself only for a business trip I had to take. I just got back. Now what's bitin' on you, Gordon?"

"Brooks delivered the horses all right." Dale spoke up quickly. Watching Strong's face and eyes he went on, "But either on his own hook or on orders from you, he took old Pete out of the bunch and substituted a tricky black outlaw. That horse was gentle to catch and saddle, but a killer at heart. He near murdered Gordon."

The ranchman stiffened, his eyebrows lifted in astonishment. "What?" Sa-ay I have got a black outlaw. Brooks spoiled him, and—"

"Why do you keep a man who spoils horses?" asked Dale.

"Because he's a good hand with sheep. Fact, he wants to get into the sheep business himself, but he hasn't any ranch. You got an idea Brooks pulled a fast one on Gordon?"

"Sure I have," said Dale and swiftly told his story.

Strong snapped, "I've been away. Let's talk to Brooks—Ho, Sid! Come here!"

The man who stepped out of the nearby stable was the same tall, lean hawkish-featured individual with whom Dale had clashed on the ridge above Gordon's ranch.

"What's wrong," he asked calmly.

Jeff Strong answered in a brittle tone. "These fellows say that either you or I, or both of us, tried to get Gordon killed by taking him my black outlaw, and that just today somebody took away the outlaw and put old Pete in Gordon's corral. Know anything about it, Sid?"

"Nope. I delivered old Pete along with the unbroke horses to Gordon, just as you told me to, Jeff," Brooks replied glibly.

Dale put in hotly, "I suppose you didn't meet

me atop that ridge and try to stop me from helping Gordon?"

Brooks gave him a cool, level look. "I never
seen you till right now."

"Why, you—" Dale smothered the rest. "Where
is the black outlaw now?" he demanded.

Strong looked at Brooks, who shrugged and
answered, "In the corral. He ain't been off the
place an hour since you left home, boss."

"Mr. Strong," Dale said eagerly, "let's ask
some of your other men to verify that."

His high hope of proving that Brooks had lied
faded out as Strong returned briefly, "My other
men are out at the line camps. Sid Brooks was
here alone while I was gone."

Gordon spoke aside to Dale, "It's no use. Let's
drop it."

Dale however was of no mind to drop it, and
whispered in return. "I believe it's only Brooks
who's guilty. He wants to run sheep, so if you
were snuffed out he'd grab your range . . . We
can't let him get away with what he's tried once.
He's sure to try again—after I've gone."

Gordon nodded. "But the stinker will stick to
his lies," he pointed out. "And he was smart
enough to switch horses before Strong got home,
so how can we prove—?"

Dale's eyebrows had drawn together over his

nose with the concentration of thought: I can't let Brooks outsmart me. Somehow I must— "Comet!" the word spouted from his lips. "We'll use Comet to show Brooks up."

Not comprehending, Gordon stared while Dale called, "Come on, everybody! Let's make the black outlaw a witness." He started toward the corral.

Strong said, "I'm beginning to think you two fellows are crazy. I can't see why you've made up this wild story. How can a horse be a witness?"

"Craziest stuff I ever heard of," Brooks agreed. "You can't prove nothin' by a horse. Horses can't talk."

"Lucky for you they can't," retorted Dale.

The other men trailed after him to Strong's corrals and there, one of a small cavvy, was the black outlaw. With his saddle rope in hand, Dale climbed the fence. "Mr. Strong, you admit that this horse," indicating Comet, "turns vicious when a man tries to ride him, and if he throws his rider, goes completely haywire and tries to kill?"

"Right," said Strong. "Leading up to what?"

Brooks' smile was derisive as he said, "But that ain't so any more. I tamed the black while you've been gone, Jeff."

Dale almost fell off the fence. Brooks had

beaten him to the punch! Dale had been going to prove to Strong that he, Dale, had tamed Comet, hoping that this would convince the ranchman that his story and Gordon's were the truth.

"*You've* tamed him?" Strong asked incredulously.

"Sure. Gentle as a kitten now. Anybody can ride 'im." Brooks pushed back his hat to grin tantalizingly at Dale.

But Dale's next words erased Brooks' grin. "Prove it! Let's see you ride Comet."

"Comet?" asked Strong, looking hard at Dale.

"Yes, sir. That's the name I gave your black outlaw while he was on Fred Gordon's ranch. I've been making out okay with him. But Sid Brooks won't dare try to ride the horse."

Strong faced Brooks, "Sid, this cowboy's put you on the spot. Get your saddle."

"Okay," said Brooks in a bored tone, and went to get his saddle.

Dale suspected the fellow believed the horse was so completely tamed he might safely ride him.

Jumping off the fence, Dale caught Comet. The black acted spooky until it smelled of Dale. Then as if reassured it quieted down.

A few minutes later, Dale noticed that Brooks' dark face showed fear and worry as he swung the saddle on Comet. Mounted, Brooks held a tight rein on the black and tried his best to coax it not to buck.

But Comet turned his head and caught the smell of his rider's leg. That was all he needed. The smell apparently drove out of his brain the training Dale had instilled into the vicious brute. Hating Brooks, Comet went crazy, bucking as he'd never bucked before and bawling every time he hit ground.

Brooks was a good rider. He stuck for five back-breaking leaps before he sailed out of the saddle and hit dust with a resounding thud. The black fury wheeled about face, and with ears flat against his poll, teeth bared, he lunged at the thrown rider.

Dale shot a glance at Strong and Gordon atop the fence. They looked to be all eyes in white, startled faces and were as unmoving as if they were petrified.

For the thousandth part of a second, Dale hesitated, his thoughts running swifter than light: Why should he risk his life to try to save Brooks? That guy deserved the fate that hung over him. But an instant later Dale hurled himself at the infuriated horse.

The time when Dale had saved Gordon from those ripping teeth and battering front feet he had been mounted, and Buttons had helped. How Buttons had helped! Now Dale was on foot beating the horse's head with his rope, catching glimpses of Brooks' agonized face as Comet's hoofs pounded him.

All at once, the black fury turned on Dale. His teeth tore at the cowboy's shoulder, and his front feet struck him down. Half-stunned, Dale lay still for an instant, trying to gather wits and strength. But he could not have escaped serious injury had not Comet pivoted back to Brooks, attacking the helpless man again, and with redoubled fury.

Dale came to his feet, dropped his useless rope, grabbed Comet's ears in his hands and with super strength given him through excitement, hung on and tried to force the brute's head down against the ground. This helped for a few seconds, until Dale felt his grip weakening. He could no longer hold those slippery ears. Frantically, he caught the bridle reins in one hand, the saddle horn in the other, bounded to Comet's back and ripped his spurs along the horse's sides and flanks. Stung by the spurs, Comet squealed defiance, bunched his hoofs, shot up into the air, and came down bucking.

There was a roaring in Dale's ears. He could

hear nothing, see nothing. Dazed, shaken, and weak, he yet had one clear thought: To stick and ride to a finish!

And he did.

Vaguely, he was aware that at last the horse had stopped close against the fence. Dale pulled himself up onto it, tied the bridle reins to a pole, then dropped down on the other side and staggered aimlessly around a bit before he blacked out.

When he came to his senses, he saw that Jeff Strong was mopping his face with a wet rag.

"All right now, son?" asked the rancher. "You sure put up a great ride. And all for a skunk like Brooks!"

Brooks was sitting on the ground, clothing ripped, face and body bruised and cut. But there was still a mean look in his eyes.

"You can't prove nothin' on me" he said thickly.

Gordon glared at him.

"No!" Strong roared, "But I know you've been playing Gordon dirt. There's only one answer to that. I'm going to beat the meanness out of you myself."

He got up and started toward Brooks, a picture of wrath. But Brooks knew what was coming. Scrambling to his feet, he headed for the bunkhouse on a run. At that Jeff Strong stopped and yelled.

"Pack your bedroll and git. Clear out of here for good. If I ever lay eyes on you again I'll finish the job that outlaw would have done on you."

Dale sat up.

"It looks to me, Mr. Strong, as if the black outlaw has settled this dirty mess."

The ranchman grinned: "Not entirely," he said. "I've got to pay you for breaking the broncs, Gordon. And I want to square things for what Brooks tried to do to you. How'd it be if I supplied a bunch of sheep, you to run 'em on shares? Sort of take Brooks' job. That way you'll soon have a flock of your own."

"Sounds great!" exclaimed Gordon. "Great!" his voice lifting almost to a shout.

"And what can I do for you, Dale?" Strong asked.

"Nothing," returned astonished Dale. "Unless—" His eyes went to Comet now standing quietly, sweat and dust streaked. "Unless you want to sell Comet to me."

"Sell him? I'm going to shoot the killer."

"Don't do it!" protested Dale. "I had him coming along fine, and I know I can tame him!"

"I believe you can at that," said Strong admiringly. "You just showed him who was boss. And how! Okay, he's yours, Dale."

Dale was still faint and shaky. But he was actually glad that he'd missed his uncle's roundup to help Fred Gordon. He'd made two new friends and had won the black outlaw for himself.

Glenn Balch

Wild Horse Roundup

Half a dozen cowboys left the ranch about daylight, their saddle horses crowded into a big truck. They would turn and twist for miles over narrow, two-rutted roads before backing up against some earthen bank to unload. Other riders would come up from the ranch with the "pratha," or gentle bunch, to meet them. That day we were after the fabled wild horses of the Owyhees.

There are several methods of catching wild horses. One, and perhaps the oldest, is with rope or lasso. For this the rider must get within a few feet of the wild one, and that is seldom easy. It requires an element of surprise and a fast bold saddle horse. It requires also a skillful roper. Too, the catch is limited to a few animals, usually not more than one or two, and these are frequently not the best. In the heat and excitement of the closeup there is little time to choose. Most runners, however, being the eternal optimists they are, carry ready lariats.

Another old method is called "creasing." It is done with high-powered rifles. The trick is to shoot the wild horse through the upper part of the neck, just nicking the vertebrae in such a manner as to cause temporary unconsciousness, during which the rider may put a halter on the animal. The big drawback is that few guns and fewer men are capable of the precision shooting required. More horses are killed outright than are captured. In recent years creasing has lost favor among true horsemen, though the rifle is still occasionally used to rid the range of troublesome animals, such as vicious stallions.

The most favored method of catching wild horses is to "trap," or corral, them. This is less wearing on both men and horses and has numerous variations, depending to some extent on the nature of the country in which the running is done. Wild horses are exceedingly wary of any enclosure, and usually some trick is necessary to get them into a trap.

A favored trick of the early days was to close one end of a canyon through which the horses were accustomed to run. Another was to construct long "wings" at each side of a corral gate. Still another was to camouflage the trap with brush and tree limbs, and many a horse-runner found, at the final and critical moment, that his camouflage wasn't good enough.

After the trap or corral is complete and ready, the big task still remains—that of getting the horses inside. This is where the "running" comes in. Usually it is done by men on horses, though in recent years there has been considerable use of light airplanes. For some reason the swooping shadow and the roar of an airplane engine at low level send the wild horses stampeding in fright, and a skillful pilot can herd them almost as accurately as a dog does sheep. Horses that eluded mounted runners for years have been captured through the use of the airplane.

But on this day the plan was to capture the wild horse by using a "pratha," from a Spanish word meaning gentle. The pratha consists of horses accustomed to being handled by men and therefore easy to manage. They will go into a corral without hesitation, having been in many times before. Our plan was to put the wild horses in with these and drive the whole bunch to the ranch, where it could be put in a strong, high-fenced corral. This can usually be done because horses are gregarious in nature, and wild ones recognize no difference between themselves and their tamer cousins. Where one goes, the others will follow—so the runners hope.

In the crisp air of early morning the cowboys unloaded their horses and tightened their cinches. They mounted and rode unhurriedly, well aware of the long day before them, to their appointed places on the big circle which was to start the drive.

The Owyhee wild horse country of north-western United States is high and rough. Originally it was a great plateau, but over the years the wind and the waters of the numerous streams have etched it deeply. The soil is dry and powdery. Rocks are everywhere, varying from big grey boulders to fields of broken shale. The principal plants are sagebrush and grass and, in the higher elevations, stunted evergreens. In winter it is a snowy, wind-swept waste; in summer it is a hot and dusty desert.

The wild horses did not choose this harsh land. They were driven to it as the stockmen and ranches spread over the more favorable territory. But once there, they quickly adjusted themselves. The scattered grasses are rich in nutriment, and the browse rises above the winter snows. The wild horses soon made this vast and lonely land their own. The deep canyons and crumbly slopes have become one of the last havens of the wild herds.

Reaching positions at the heads of the various long ridges, the cowboys started the drive downward. In the early part of such drives it is the wild horse's own wariness that is most helpful. Nothing more than the appearance of a rider on the skyline is usually sufficient to start him moving. The stallion will gather his mares, and the whole bunch will start away, not in fright but just in caution. That is just what the rider, holding to his ridge, wants. That the band may be a mile or more ahead of him is of no concern. The time for pressure will come later.

Indeed, some think of wild horses as they do of deer and elk, as a product of a continuously wild existence. That is not true. All the horses in America come from domesticated stock. The great wild herds of history, when thousands upon thousands of horses roamed the southwestern plains, came from animals escaped from the Spanish conquistadores. For many generations, even centuries in time, they were wild, leading lives of complete freedom, but the domestication of the Old World was in their veins. Their sires and dams had pulled the royal coaches and the two-wheeled carts of Europe, had carried armored knights in jousting tournaments.

Among the wild horses as we know them today,

it is doubtful if there are any in whom the "wild" strain has been unbroken for more than a few generations. Domestic horses escaped from the ranches are constantly infiltrating into the wild bands, adding both new blood and numbers.

But let the true wild horse lover be not one bit dismayed by that. The spooky instinct is strong in every colt and, unless overcome early, may develop into a dominating characteristic. Many a rancher has learned to his sorrow that a well-broken using horse which he turned out for a few weeks of "grass" soon became the wildest of the wild. Runners know from experience that escaped ranch horses are often the wiliest, the most stubborn, and the hardest to catch. The wild instinct in horses will never die as long as they have the freedom of the open range in which to live and reproduce.

Where then is the line? What separates the wild horse from his domestic brother? The symbol accepted by the ranchers and stockmen is the brand, and it is probably as good as any. If a horse is branded, he is owned and therefore "tame," no matter if he never has had a saddle on; if he is unbranded, he is unowned and "wild." You can have him if you are horseman enough to catch him. It is that simple.

The brand, in range country, is everything. If

the animal is of an age to leave its mother and is unbranded, then it is a "slick," or wild. If still with the mother, then the mother's brand is evidence of ownership. In the event the mother herself is unbranded, then both are slicks. In bygone days a good many hard riders built up sizeable possessions by the simple process of catching and branding slicks.

But does that slight scar on the hide, or the absence of it, make any difference in the breaking corral? Not in the least. The branded horse may well put up the longest and hardest fight. Wildness in its true sense is based on individual characteristics as well as environment and past experience. Some of the gentlest, most dependable, and best all-around horses I know came from the range bands. On the other hand, there are horses raised in stalls and man-fed all their lives to whom I would hesitate to turn my back. Brands are certainly no guarantee of temperament, or vice versa.

Coming down the ridges, the cowboys on the ends of the drive forge to the front, thus tightening the big circle. The bands of horses, still far in front of the riders, trickle together and mingle. The stallions challenge each other and even pause long enough to make a show of fighting.

One stallion, now far below his accustomed

range, turns and watches the riders. Presently he quits the others and heads at right angles across a ridge. Five or six mares with their colts and a couple of yearlings turn to follow him. But in the next draw he finds other horses, all drifting downward. Above, also, are two riders who draw together in anticipation of his intention. He watches them briefly, then turns downward with the others.

The riders know this black stallion well. They have had him in the circle before. Big, trim, and sleek, he could be a stallion of the legends. He has feet hardened by the Owyhee shale and legs tempered by the steep slopes. His heart and lungs were developed by the high thin air, and his eyes were keen as an antelope's from constant surveillance. In his mind there was a distrust of anything connected with man. He didn't like what was happening, but the herd instinct is strong and he drifted on downward with the others.

Now the slopes below the riders were alive with horses. Branded horses had been picked up along with the slicks. They moved down the draws, flowing together when they met. A fine dust haze climbed into the sunlit air.

Watching from the pratha, we could now distinguish the colors: the blacks and bays, the greys and the roans, the whites and the pintos. We could see the young colts trotting anxiously after their mothers.

An old mare was out in front in one draw, leading a herd of fifteen or twenty. She had a brand but was one of the wildest. She had won the confidence of the others by her shrewdness in the past. Now they followed willingly.

At another place a dozen or so horses have split off to the left led by another nervous mare. A rider swings wide and puts his horse to a gallop. The errant horses halt, watch him for a few seconds with lifted heads. He is still a quarter of a mile away, but his purpose is plain. The horses turn and hurry after the others.

The tempo of the whole scene has now quickened. The driven horses are moving at a trot. Their heads are up and they are alert. Behind, the riders have closed in and are pressing forward. The two wing men are well up on the sides.

We have been holding the pratha, keeping it well bunched and quiet. Now those on the upper side fade back, leaving the area between the gentle horses and the driven bunches clear. Soon the old lead mare sees the pratha. She whinnies querulously. Horses in the pratha answer. She heads for them, assured by their undisturbed manner.

There is some distrust among the others, though. They slow up and look around. Now the riders crowd up from behind, shouting and swinging ropes. This is a critical time, the time to scare them and take advantage of the herd instinct.

They move on. The front end of the drive reaches the pratha and the horses began to mingle. The riders who disappeared now come back along the sides.

But it isn't to be that easy. Instinct or something tells the black stallion that here is danger, trickery. The men are too close. He wheels back, coming at a run. Half a dozen or so of the mares break with him, young colts running by the sides of three. The stallion sees an open place in the line and heads for it. Quickly the riders spur over the rocky ground to turn him back. They are there first. The stallion changes direction, running at full tilt. Once more the men are successful in heading him. He comes around with a snort and takes off in the other direction. Now it is a race. A cowboy on a good bay horse is going all out. For a few seconds the bay holds his own, then he begins to lose ground. In desperation the cowboy jerks his rope from the saddle horn, but he is never close enough for a throw.

The riders have pulled their sweat-dripping

horses to a halt. They know now that it is useless, that they are beaten. Once the stallion got above them, they could not hope to head him.

The stallion knew it, too. He soon slowed his pace to a walk, stopped, and whinnied back to the four mares and two colts that had filtered through the line in the excitement. Then he turned and toiled slowly back up the long ridge to the high green range that he loved. The mares and colts followed.

"Well," one of the cowboys said, "he cleaned us again." But there was a touch of admiration in his voice, for the black was unconquerable that day.

By now the wild horses and the gentle ones were in a common herd, but the range horses were milling about nervously.

"Come on," the rancher said. "Let's get started, or we'll be losing some more."

Two riders struck out for the ranch at a trot. The rest of us crowded the herd from the upper side. It bulged in the center and was soon strung out after the point riders. We kept it moving at a merry clip across the big, dusty flat. The wild ones were a little jittery, but the movement kept them from getting ideas.

At a break in a crumbly rim, the two point men turned downward. Below in the stream's bottom

lay the ranch, with its fenced fields and network
of pole corrals. At the rim the wild ones sought to
pause, tried to break back to the dusty sage. We
who were behind drove forward, crowding them,
yelling and swinging ropes. They stood it for a few
seconds; then the herd spilled over the edge and
flowed downward in a plunging, dust-swirling
stream.

Soon they were in a lane between two fields,
where there was no turning back. The two point
riders raced on, opening gates. The gentle ones
trotted willingly enough, for these corrals were
home to them. The wild ones could do nothing
but follow. Soon they were in a big corral.

The rancher dismounted and climbed the fence
to select the ones he wanted to keep up for breaking or sale. "That bay there," he said, "looks like
saddle stock to me."

The next day the young colts were branded.
Then, along with the mares and the others not to
be kept, they were turned back to the high range,
to roam in peaceful freedom until another roundup.

D. S. Halacy, Jr.

Ride the Rough String

Clyde Bowman watched
the big gray horse as he drove the remuda along
toward the line camp. Jigger was a lot of animal;
big-muscled and cat-eyed, with hair-trigger action when a man got into the saddle. Getting to
go along with Steve McCullough on this hunt for
strays was a break for Clyde. Not many fifteen-
year-olds were that lucky. And to have Jigger
along among the half-dozen mounts they brought
with them for the two weeks of combing the canyons was more than Clyde had hoped for. Now,
at last, he'd get to ride the gray, and wait till he
told the kids back in town!

"There's camp, kid," Steve said, motioning up
ahead. Almost at the base of the ridge knifing up
from the desert, Clyde made out the low building

that was the bunkhouse. Off to the right were the posts of the corral.

"It's about time," he said, tipping back his hat and rubbing his arm across his forehead. "Seems like we've been riding a week."

"Try walking her some time!" Steve said. "That'll take you a real week. Near twenty-five miles, I reckon." He laughed softly and started to whistle "Sweet Bessie," holding his horse to the same easy walk.

"Can't we let 'em out a little, Steve?" Clyde asked. He was eager to get to the camp. The sun was still two hours over the hills; there'd be time for what he wanted to do.

"Ride out, kid," Steve said, amusement in his voice. "I'll bring the cavvy along."

"I'll get them there," Clyde said. "I'm going to put my saddle on old Jigger and show him who's boss before sundown, Steve. I've been waiting for this a long time."

"You'll wait a mite longer, I figure, kid," Steve said. "I'll ride Jigger this trip."

"But you've got to let me," Clyde pleaded, reining close to Steve.

He had been sure the lean puncher wouldn't be like the boss back at the home ranch. "Didn't I braid you that riata? And how about all those trips I made to town for you?"

The wrinkles around Steve's eyes deepened, and some of the humor left his gray eyes. There was even a different tone to his voice. It was almost like that of Clyde's father.

"How old are you, kid?" he asked.

Clyde clamped his jaws together hard, looking away from the cowboy. It was the old trap, the one Steve hadn't used for months. No matter what he answered, Clyde would lose either way. A long time ago, when he first came to the Rafter B, Steve had stung him on it. Clyde had answered fourteen, proudly, and Steve had laughed and said, "You're too young for your wants to hurt you!" And the next time it had been, "Old enough to know better, kid!" So now Clyde kept his mouth tight shut.

The details of the line camp grew. Clyde could make out the chimney and see that the corral was empty, but there was no eagerness in him now to get there. For two cents, he thought, he'd wheel the old mare they let him ride and head back. If they were going to treat him like a baby all his life, what was the use?

"Nobody home, kid," Steve said, his voice pleasant again. "I was sort of hoping for company. Gets mighty lonesome out here." Clyde said nothing, keeping his eyes straight to the front. His jaw muscles were so tight they hurt. Steve started to whistle again and they finished the ride to the line camp without any more talk.

"Throw the mounts in the corral, kid," Steve said, swinging down and loosening the saddle on his horse. "I'll get busy with some grub. We got a choice. You want beans or spuds?"

"Suit yourself," Clyde answered, climbing down tiredly to open the gate. "Don't look like I've got any say-so around this place." Grimly he ran the horses into the corral, then checked the trough to make sure they had water. Jigger snorted when another horse ran against him, rearing high. There was still plenty of life and kick in the gray, even after the all-day trip.

In the fading light, Clyde leaned against the fence rails, watching the gray smoke snake up from the bunkhouse chimney. It wasn't fair, he told himself—not fair at all. For a year now he had done all the dirty jobs, mended fences and dug ditches. He could ride, and yet they treated him like a no-good wrangler who couldn't be trusted.

Well, two weeks was a long time. With just the two of them here, a lot could happen. He'd ride Jigger before he got back to the home ranch. He'd show them all if he was too young or not.

Steve hollered "Supper!" from the bunkhouse

and Clyde sighed and walked slowly toward the smell of beans and bacon. He wasn't hungry, but he'd better eat.

There was another disappointment in the morning. Steve told him to stay in camp for the first two days, while the cowboy went north into the canyons, looking for Rafter B stock.

"That's rough country, kid," he said. "I'll make better time by my lonesome. When we loop south, you can go along. Meantime, you see the horses are all right. You might clean up the bunk-house some, and have some grub going when I get back day after tomorrow."

"Thanks a million," Clyde said bitterly. "I should have figured something like this. All I'm good for is mucking out boar's nests, huh? Sure you trust me to cook for you?"

Steve's eyes went steel-hard, and he turned in the doorway to face the boy. The angry look on his face hurt, too, because Clyde had thought the puncher was his friend and wanted to give him every break he could.

"Look, boy," Steve said, his voice like a honed knife, "you're getting a mite too big for them britches. A man don't learn to ride in the year you've been with us. I get no kick out of telling you off; but it's for your own good, understand?"

Clyde looked at his boots, chewing on his lip without answering the puncher.

"And one more thing," Steve went on. "Don't get any notion about riding that Jigger horse, either. I'd take him along with me, but he's a poor horse for the stuff I'll be riding over. Ride any of the others, but keep off Jigger. If I'm not back by Friday, you better ride out looking for me. I'll see you."

Clyde watched him go, riding the paint and leading Clyde's old mare for a pack horse. Steve flung up an arm as he cleared the corral, but the boy didn't answer the wave. He watched until the puncher disappeared up the tortuous canyon, then walked over to the corral.

Picking up a pebble, he flipped it lightly at the gray horse, smiled stiffly when the animal threw back its head and pawed the ground.

"Go on," he said aloud. "Kick up all you want to. I'll ride you, and it might be sooner than you think."

The pipe that fed the trough from the small spring outside the corral was clogged and the water level had dropped fast with the horses drinking thirstily. Clyde knew he ought to clean it out, but there was time for that later.

Same way about cleaning the bunkhouse. If

Steve had said nothing, he would have gotten right to work. But now, he decided he'd take his own sweet time about it. There was no hurry, the lanky rider wouldn't be back for two days. This was Clyde's chance to take it easy.

In the afternoon, he climbed the ridge and used the field glasses he'd brought. There was no sign of Steve—the rider was far to the north, coaxing strays out of blind canyons when they had drifted from the flatland.

Back at the corral, Clyde went inside, swinging his rope and grinning at the gray horse. Something banged behind him, and he turned to see the corral gate swing wide open. Snorting, he dropped the rope and hurried back to shut the gate in time. Steve would skin him alive if he let the remuda break out!

With the rope going again, he approached the skittish gray. His loop went true, settling over Jigger's head. He got a dally around the snubbing post and, seconds later, had his jacket over the horse's head. Unable to see, Jigger stood nervously. "What was hard about this?" Clyde thought exultantly. Five minutes later, he had the saddle on the gray, and, with his heart beating wildly, he got a foot in the stirrup and swung aboard.

"No hurry," he said aloud. "I've got lots of time, Jigger, old horse. I'll finish the job tomorrow!" At his words, the animal shook and snorted, tossing his big head in an effort to rid himself of the jacket. Clyde felt the power and wildness under him, but it was a challenge he had to meet.

Swinging down, he loosened his rope, pulled the jacket free and vaulted the fence, with Jigger right back of him. Safe on the outside, he laughed at the big horse. He'd show him who was the boss, after all.

He felt so good then that he got busy and cleaned out the bunkhouse, even airing the bedding. After that, he got at the water pipe, and then it was time for supper.

By lamplight, he read the torn magazines until his eyes grew heavy. Then he rolled into bed and blew out the lamp. He went to sleep happy. Tomorrow was the day. Steve or no Steve, Clyde would saddle Jigger and ride him out of the corral. Then he could tell them he was old enough!

Clyde took his time, relishing the treat that was in prospect. After breakfast, he roped out old Dynamite, the Roman-nosed bay, and rode him up the ridge. From the crest, he swept the country to the north with the field glasses again. There was no sign of Steve, and Clyde rode back down to camp, grinning expectantly.

Opening the corral gate, he hazed all the horses

but Jigger to the far end. Jigger didn't haze much, but that was all right. Clyde repeated yesterday's session, snubbing the gray and tying the jacket over his head. Only this time, instead of just climbing down, he eyed the open gate, anchored his spurs in the cinches and threw the jacket to one side!

He had it all figured out. If he couldn't shut the gate as he went out, it wouldn't make much difference. The water trough would keep the remuda close by. And if they strayed, he could round them up on Jigger.

Trouble was, Jigger hadn't been let in on Clyde's plans. The gray exploded like a blasting charge when he could see. One leap and the boy dropped the hat that he had planned to fan the gray with. On the second jump, it seemed that Clyde was looking up at the ground, and the fence was a blur of posts.

He didn't have the reins any more, and both hands fought each other for purchase on the saddle horn. Jigger took it on himself to slam full tilt into the rest of the horses at the far end of the corral, and that was when Clyde lost the stirrups. At the bottom of a wild, pinwheeling leap, his jaws cracked together so hard he thought he could feel his teeth popping out!

"Hang on!" he told himself desperately. "Tire

him out!" But suddenly there was nothing under him but air. The ground spun in a crazy slant, driving up at him, then everything went black.

How long he had been chewing sand, he didn't know. Blinking his eyes, he turned his head, trying to focus on something. Slowly his vision steadied. There were the fence posts, with the bunkhouse beyond. With an effort, Clyde gathered his arms under him and pushed up from the ground.

His body was one big bruise, and it even hurt to breathe. But he forgot that as his eyes swept the corral. There wasn't a horse left in it! Groaning and spitting sand, he staggered up. Far to the south was a boiling wake of dust. Jigger had spooked the rest of the remuda, and they had followed him!

Hobbling painfully, Clyde came to the jacket he had tied over Jigger. The trough was beyond it, and he moved toward it, thinking to wash the dust and sand from his bleeding face. The bottom was wet, but that was all. The pipe must have clogged again; no wonder the horses had followed Jigger out.

It seemed a mile to the bunkhouse, but he made it, and at last he had himself looking human again. How he could feel so banged up with no broken bones was a mystery. Worse than that was the worry about what he could do now. The horses would likely gallop for miles, at least until Jigger found water. Clyde's chances of running them down were mighty slim.

Climbing the ridge was agony, but he made it. With the glasses, he tried to spot the horses to the south, but couldn't. He had really done it now! When Steve came back—quickly he swung the glasses to the north, feeling a guilty dread. With relief, he saw no horse. Then he saw the man, moving slowly down out of the canyon!

A frown wrinkled Clyde's forehead. Who would be afoot in the rough country? The white hat told him. It was Steve. Clyde's heart quickened its beat. The puncher must be in trouble. No cowboy walked unless—Clyde moved down the ridge as fast as he could, and then headed north toward where he had seen the creeping figure.

He met the cowboy two miles from the bunkhouse, and he ran the last hundred yards after he made out the blood caking Steve's face. The puncher staggered and fell as Clyde reached him.

"Panther," Steve gasped. "Jumped the old mare. I was riding back to try to shoot the varmint when my horse broke a leg. I . . ."

"Take it easy, Steve," Clyde said, bending over the fallen cowboy to shade him from the sun.

Steve must have taken a bad fall, his face was torn and bleeding, and his shirt was matted with blood. "Your chest . . ."

"I busted something, kid," Steve said hoarsely. "Sorry I pulled such a bonehead trick. You . . ." The rest was lost in a long, tired sigh as Steve passed out.

On his knees in the dust, Clyde looked at the distant bunkhouse. It might as well have been a hundred miles, for all his chances of getting Steve to it. There was a clump of mesquite ten yards off. The shade of that would be better than nothing. Carefully, he dragged Steve toward it.

The rider's breathing was ragged and labored, and when Clyde touched his head, it was hot with fever. Steve needed help, and bad. In near panic, Clyde thought of the horses he had let out. What a fool he had been! They were right, Steve and the boss and the others. He was a kid, without a brain in his head. And now he had let the cowboy down.

For a long moment he bowed his head, praying fervently. When he lifted it, he got to his feet, trying not to notice the pain in his legs and arms. He had paid a big price for riding Jigger. He couldn't let Steve pay a bigger one.

He left a note under the canteen and grub he put alongside the puncher. The note said to sit tight while Clyde went for help. It was a blessing Steve didn't know how Clyde went, on shank's mare, his rope slung over one shoulder.

The boy walked until dark with the prayer on his lips that he would have the chance to prove himself a man, that Jigger would show up somewhere along the way, and that this time he would cling on his back.

After dark he realized there was another way to prove himself—a harder way, a killing way. Keeping the Pole Star on his right, he walked on mile after mile. When he couldn't walk another step, he jogged.

The faint hope stayed with him a long time and it was near morning when he flung down the rope. For a mile that helped, even shedding its slight weight. His feet burned as though his boots were filled with live coals and he knew that if he stopped he would never start again, his muscles were that tight. So he kept on.

Clyde Bowman was a kid of fifteen when he left the unconscious cowboy and struck out afoot for the home ranch. He was a man when he stumbled onto the porch and beat his doubled fist against the door. He was man enough that he pulled himself into a saddle and rode back with the doctor and the boss, to be sure Steve McCullough was all right. After that, he slept for twelve hours on the floor, with the boots the doctor had cut from his swollen feet lying there beside him.

"Evenin', Clyde." It was Steve, bandaged from his waist to his neck but somehow able to hold a coffee cup. And even in the flickering shadows of the bunkhouse, Clyde could see that the puncher was grinning at him. "Thanks for bailing me out of a tight one."

"I didn't do anything," Clyde said. "Outside of make a fool of myself. You were right about Jigger, I guess."

"Speaking of that brute," the boss said from the table, "he's back in the corral, Clyde. Came traipsin' in a while ago, with the rest of the runaways in tow. You aim to ride him south for strays?" There was a good-natured twinkle in his eyes, and he smiled as he waited for Clyde to answer.

"I'll think on it," Clyde said easily. "Seems like now I'm all of a sudden old enough so I'm in no big hurry!"

And while the others laughed, he grinned at his ruined boots. He'd ride the gray, all right—when it was time.

Carl Henry Rathjen

The Curb Bit

Would this night never end? For the tenth time eleven-year-old George Washington opened his eyes. Then he saw the October dawn pushing back the blanket of darkness. He rolled eagerly out of bed and began to dress hurriedly.

This was not just an ordinary Saturday. Today he had a special reason for getting up early. Secret plans to make this Saturday in 1743 better than any he had ever known.

Then, in his excitement, he dropped a boot. *Clump!* It resounded through the two-story red house on the east bank of the Rappahannock River. George held his breath, wondering if his older half-brothers, Lawrence and Augustine, had arrived here at Stafford late last night. If they connected the sound to his room at this time of morning, they'd want to know what was afoot.

Listening for approaching footsteps, George considered whether to jump back into bed and pretend to be sleeping or try to have another man-to-man talk with them? He would be tactful but bold. He would say, "Since Father's death you've been more than good to me, trying to take his place. But you're treating me like a child instead of a young man—"

He knew just how they would interrupt.

"We'll discuss that after we discover what escapade you're planning. It's probably something to make us consider sending you off to school for disciplining."

So he would have to call their attention to certain rights.

"My place is here. You've inherited *your* estates, Mount Vernon and Wakefield, so why can't I have the freedom of Stafford? After all, I'm to be its master, according to Father's will."

They would laugh and remind him that he wasn't of age. That day was a long way off, according to them.

George sighed. That's the way it always went. But evidently it wouldn't go like that today, because the house remained silent. Either they weren't here or they hadn't heard the boot.

He finished dressing, quietly, then eased into the dim upper hall, and tiptoed past his mother's door. She couldn't understand his love of dangerous activities either. She refused to recognize that, despite his years, he was big and powerful—a young man ready to meet the dangers that were the task and duty of every young gentleman worth his salt in His Majesty's Colony of Virginia.

Well, he'd show them today. If not in years, then in ability and behavior. So, as befitted the future master of Stafford, he was going to ride after the hounds with other gentry of the countryside. He was going to attend his first fox-hunt.

Outside the house he paused to gaze down the gently sloping meadow to the river, the way a master would survey his estate on a fine morning. And it *was* going to be a perfect day for the fox-hunt—air as crisp as the dry leaves underfoot and sharp enough to make the baying of the hounds bugle through scarlet woods; just enough frost in the earth to make the horses' hoofs ring. A wonderful day to be alive.

But a wasted day if he didn't obtain a hunter from the stables before someone surmised his plans. Abandoning the gentlemanly manner, he ran until suddenly he saw the mounted figure of Trance, the plantation overseer, riding to intercept him. George slowed his pace. What should he do about Trance when he became master of

Stafford? The man was an excellent manager, but in some ways a bit too harsh to suit George.

"Good morning, Mr. Trance," George said with cheery casualness.

The burly overseer reined in and touched the brim of his hat with the coiled bull whip he always carried.

"Morning, Master George." His dark eyes twinkled. "It looks as if you're headed toward the stables again."

It sounded friendly, but that word "again" made George feel he should be on guard.

"It's a fine morning for a bit of a canter," he remarked, then stopped short as the overseer swung his horse to bar the way. He fought down the temper he had inherited from his father, but he wouldn't be stared down.

"Master George," the overseer said reluctantly, "you're spending more time at the stables than your father ever permitted."

Lawrence and Augustine had frequently remarked about that, too. George wondered how, when they were away so much, they knew so much about his doings.

"Mr. Trance," George inquired, "did my mother or brothers give you orders to stop me?"

If they had, he would have to obey. The overseer answered slowly.

"They haven't gotten around to it yet," he said, but he didn't move his horse. George felt his face becoming icy, the way it always did just before . . . "However," Trance continued quickly, "I know what's in their minds, so for your own good I'll tell you."

"Mr. Trance!" George's temper took the bit in its teeth. "You're forgetting I'm to be master of this estate!"

The overseer stared, then chuckled. Next he laughed. Then he guffawed, slapping his thigh with the coiled whip.

"You think *you're* going to run things?" he gasped. George's face became hot. Some of the heat transferred to his tongue.

"I'll give you one of my future orders right now. If you're wise, you'll obey it in advance of my becoming master of Stafford."

The overseer leaned from the saddle and looked as though he couldn't decide whether to be amused or angry.

"And what would that order be?"

"It's about the constant appearance of that whip in your hand," George snapped. "From now on I don't want to see you using it any more on man or beast."

Trance had a reasonable reply.

"Some of the horses, such as you try to ride, my

lad, need it till they're more than half-trained. And the slaves often need it."

The reference to his riding ability stung George, and he had to admit to himself that Trance never used the whip on any of the help unless they goaded him to it. He also wondered if the overseer were merely trying to tease him. All this irritated him. Then, in the distance up the river, he heard a hound bugling. It would soon be time for the hunt. Still, he was master, and he did not approve of the whip.

"I meant what I said about that whip, Mr. Trance."

"Young George," the overseer was losing his good nature. "I take orders from your mother when your brother Lawrence isn't around." He pointedly shook out the coils. "And if you were my son or younger brother, I'd let you feel some of this lash instead."

George forgot the hunt and stepped toward him. But Trance swung his horse around, then reined in a few paces away.

"Son, you have much to learn before you become master of Stafford. You could learn it here, instead of at school, but you'll keep on pushing the patience of me and your brothers until—"

He shrugged, then cantered away through the fallen autumn leaves. George stared after him.

So that was it! He had often mentioned Trance's whip to his brothers. He thought they had ignored him, but evidently they hadn't. Perhaps Trance had made up stories to them about their younger brother. Maybe that's why they always took such an exasperated attitude toward everything he did. And another thing, if he were sent off to school— instead of continuing with a tutor—Trance would have almost complete freedom in managing Stafford. In fact, he would practically be its master!

George decided he'd better insist on having a real man-to-man talk with his brothers. But meanwhile, there was the fox-hunt. He hurried on his way to the stables.

In the gangway between the stalls he came face to face with a big, intensely black man.

"Sampson," he greeted his father's favorite trainer of horses, "I'm planning to attend the hunt this morning." He could confide in Sampson who had soft understanding ways with animals and humans. George motioned eagerly toward a stall. "How about that sorrel?"

Sampson's dark face became troubled.

"Massa George, Massa Trance would not like it."

The overseer's name spurred George's temper again.

"That horse belongs to the estate, not to Mr. Trance."

"But—"

"Sampson!" George curbed himself. It wasn't like Sampson to oppose him. Even when teaching horsemanship, the trainer always made his corrections unobtrusively. There must be some good reason for his more direct, odd behavior this morning. "What is it, Sampson? Isn't that sorrel in condition for hunting?"

"Oh, he's fit, Massa George, full of spirit."

"Then why—"

"It's just what Massa Trance told me—"

"Saddle the horse!" George snapped, then felt suddenly contrite for his curt manner. Sampson was accustomed to kindness, and he took great pride in the fact that he had never been whipped by tongue or lash. George spoke apologetically. "I'm not angry at you, Sampson. I realize you have orders from Mr. Trance, but he takes his from me. We have just had an understanding about it."

Sampson's deep eyes looked worriedly indecisive a moment.

"I'll ready the sorrel, Massa George," he said quietly. A little too quietly, George thought uncomfortably, as he hurried to change into clothes he had brought to the stable last night.

As he approached the big sorrel, it pawed the ground restively and looked more spirited than any horse he had ridden before. But he liked the excitement and possible danger of it. Sampson kept a firm grip on the snaffle rein.

"Massa George, I'll adjust yo' stirrups after you mount."

George noticed that the left iron hung extra long so he could mount without help, like a man. Good old Sampson! George gathered in the curb and snaffle reins. Sampson reached for the stirrup leather. The sorrel lunged forward.

"Whoa!" George commanded, hauling on the curb bit. The horse flung up its head and reared. George spurred him down. Sampson seized the bridle again.

"Slo-o-o-w, boy," he said soothingly. "Yo'all is foolish not savin' yo'self for. followin' the hounds." He looked up, the morning sun sheening his smiling face. "Massa George, hold him soft-like. He's got a bit of temper in his spirit, an' if you curb it too sharp, he rears hisself into trouble."

George wondered if Sampson did not intend the remark to apply to himself as well as the horse. Sampson, busy with the stirrup, still talked softly.

"Just enough curb so's he don't try to get bossy

an' take the bit in his teeth. That way he'll learn
it's easier to move along comfortablelike. Ain't no
sense in bein' so tight-reined everybody gets
fightin' mad, 'cause that only means somebody's
spirit gets broke." Sampson smiled up again, but
his eyes seemed a little sad. "Good luck an' good
huntin', Massa George."

"Thanks, Sampson," George replied, still wondering. Then the sorrel bolted from the stable-
yard, nearly unseating him. He let the hunter go
as though that had been his intention, not the
horse's. Maybe Sampson had been trying to warn
him he didn't ride well enough yet for a powerful
horse like this.

But he couldn't go back now and ask Sampson
to choose a horse for him. Besides, he didn't want
to. The more fighting spirit in a horse, the better.
A young gentleman of the Virginia Colony had to
learn to face danger. Indians lurked about, and
Frenchmen had their greedy eyes on land west of
the Alleghenies which rightfully belonged to
Britain. A future officer of His Majesty's Army
couldn't let himself be intimidated by a mere
horse.

Trying to rein in to a brisk trot, George used
too much curb again. The sorrel tossed its head
furiously, reared, felt the spurs, and jolted down
into another mad gallop. Somehow George man-

aged to stay in the saddle. Not frightened. But angry. Yet he remembered Sampson had always told him never to lose his temper with an animal.

Curbing his anger, George slowly brought the horse under control, though it was hard to maintain because in the crisp air the sorrel wanted to go . . . go . . go. George and the horse were in a tense sweat when they arrived at the estate where other huntsmen were gathered. He saw nudges and knowing smiles, probably because he was a Washington and his family was somewhat looked down upon by other Virginians who considered themselves to be superior gentry. Then he overheard some of the remarks.

"Rather a big horse for a little fellow to try to stay on."

Just like home. His brothers, Trance, Sampson.

"Sir," George replied, keeping his voice calm, "I shall still be mounted when the hounds run a fox to earth."

"If he doesn't run away with you," another gentleman suggested.

George flushed, recalling how close the sorrel had come to achieving the upper hand during the four-mile ride from home. But he smiled and said:

"Are you planning your alibi, sir, for when we show you our heels? The Washington horses are extremely fast and spirited."

An older man rode close.

"That's the kind of challenge to silence ridicule."

George smiled appreciatively as the man swung away. Sampson had been right. You did get along more comfortably when you didn't let your temper have full rein. Maybe it would be worth a try on his brothers and Trance.

Then the hunt moved out slowly. Suddenly the hounds no longer nosed about. They went into full cry as a red fox fled from beneath a bush, streaked under a fence, and sped across a meadow. A huntsman's horn sounded. Horses' hoofs drummed in pursuit.

George let the sorrel have its head, determined to make good on his challenge to the other hunters. But his horse tried to turn aside from the first jump. George checked him barely in time to clear the fence awkwardly. Someone laughed.

Approaching a hedgerow, George tightened the reins, but too much, forcing the sorrel to take off too slowly. The horse came down astraddle the hedge. Other riders laughed, sailing over. George angrily spurred his horse clear of the hedge.

Pounding after the other hunters, the sorrel shook its head. George eased the reins a trifle. The horse soared smoothly over a stone wall. Then a brook. A rick-rack fence. Down a gully.

Up the far side. They were neck and neck with the leaders now, right there on the scene with everyone else when the houndsman held aloft the brushy tail of the fox.

On the next chase George and the sorrel had no trouble with the snaffle and curb bits. Not too tight nor too loose, but just right for perfect control to stay on the heels of the hounds ahead of the field.

Then the hunt was over. The sorrel was scarcely winded, still keyed up and full of fighting spirit. And George was full of exultation. He had ridden the hunt.

"All right," George cried. "Go ahead and take the bit in your teeth. But I'm warning you, when you're tired and want to stop, I'll keep going and teach you a lesson."

So, heading home cross-country, he let the sorrel go! He didn't know whether Sampson would approve of his tactics. But no matter. What could compare to the excitement and danger of this fast, thrilling ride? Tearing across meadow. Down dale. Rail fences. Rock walls. Hedgerows.

In a grove, deer scattered before the wild dash of the sorrel. From a pond ducks rose with wildly flapping wings. Gray squirrels scampered up tree trunks and screamed indignantly. George laughed.

Ahead he spotted a sunken bubbling brook. It didn't look like a good spot to cross, but since the horse had its head, there was no time to change matters now. He felt the sorrel gather itself for a mighty lunge. The brook whisked back beneath the reaching horse. On the far bank the sorrel's hoofs scattered crackling dry leaves, then struck mud beneath them. A wild slip. George drew in the reigns sharply, making the hunter fight to stay on its feet.

"Good boy," he cried. Now the horse had had enough. It slackened pace abruptly. "Oh, no, you don't," George reminded, giving a touch of spurs. Then he saw the sharp rise and fall of the horse's head as it tried to respond. George quickly dismounted. The sorrel was lame! They would both have to walk home because the sorrel had been given the freedom of its head.

It was a long trip, with nothing exciting about it. Not with a painfully limping horse and riding boots that weren't designed for hiking. George was doing some blistered limping of his own when, along toward noon, he finally reached Stafford.

Seeing a group of grooms outside the stable courtyard, he called for them to take the horse. They didn't hear him as they stared into the courtyard. He called again. They turned frightened dark faces, then peered into the yard again as a groom hurried to George and the sorrel.

"Someone having trouble with a horse in there?" George inquired. He didn't really care, too footsore for any more excitement.

"No, suh," the groom answered as George turned away. "It . . . it's Massa Trance. H-he say he gonna whip S-Sampson for givin' dis sorrel out."

George paused, tempted to go on up to the house as though he hadn't heard. Sampson would take the blame for whatever the trouble was about the sorrel. He could keep silent, and George's brothers would never know the true circumstances.

But George spun around. Sampson was a Mandingo, a member of an immensely proud tribe, who would not be able to bear the humiliation of a whipping. But more than that he had been a friend, a patient teacher of horsemanship.

George dashed into the courtyard just as Trance, facing a resigned Sampson, swung the whip back for the first blow. George caught the lash and yanked it from the surprised overseer's grasp.

"Trance," he snapped, his face flushing, "I told you earlier not to use this whip any more."

"I don't take orders from a boy," Trance

retorted.

That stung, too.

"If you're convinced of that," George challenged, "you may have your whip . . . if you can take it from me."

The overseer glowered.

"That's disciplining your brothers will have to handle. So mind your own troubles, Master George, and give me the whip."

George deliberately coiled it.

"There *will* be trouble if I allow you to whip Sampson."

That seemed to make Trance realize what he had been about to do. He looked startled. But his voice was still harsh.

"There'll be trouble either way. Sampson had no right to give you the sorrel. I'd informed him that your brother Lawrence had sold it."

"Mr. Trance," he began quietly, "Sampson tried to tell me, but I *made* him give me the horse."

Just then a groom led the limping sorrel into the yard.

"Lame!" Trance exploded. "And the buyer, coming this afternoon, wanted that horse for immediate use. Now the sale will be lost and probably my job with it, thanks to Sampson." Trance's voice rose. "He should have told you. Give me that whip!"

George pushed him back, more in restraint than defiance.

"Don't make me lose my temper, Mr. Trance. *I* insisted on that horse. *I* brought it in lame. *I'm* responsible for the loss of the sale. Not you or Sampson."

Trance began to look relieved, but he was doubtful.

"If you tell your brother, you know what that means."

"I'll be sent away to school for disciplining just as you tried to tell me for my own good earlier this morning." George knew now he'd been wrong about the overseer, about himself, about a lot of things. He motioned to the grooms peering around the corner of the stable. "They can be your witnesses. But you won't need them, because I'll tell my brother the truth. And," he added pointedly, handing the whip over, "you won't need this."

For a moment he thought he had been rash in returning the whip because Trance, studying him, shook it out threateningly. Then the overseer's glance included everyone in the yard.

"There will be no mention of this, not one word to Mistress Washington or to Masters Lawrence and Augustine. Is that clear?"

The tense grooms nodded quickly. Sampson also nodded slowly.

"Master George," said Trance, relaxing, "if I can't persuade the buyer into taking some other horse, then perhaps your brother may learn that the sorrel lamed himself—" Trance smiled "—while enjoying the freedom of the pasture."

George stared. This was the man he had let himself believe was betraying him to his brothers.

"Thank you, Mr. Trance, but . . . but I don't think we should make up a falsehood to tell Lawrence."

"Very well, Master George. I hope things work out for the best, for your sake. But," Trance shook his head, "I'm afraid that, aside from this morning . . ."

"I know," George murmured. "I had more freedom of Stafford from my brothers, and you, than my father ever permitted." He was silent, thinking that they really hadn't been as strict as his father. But he'd let that temper of his convince him they were curbing him too much. So he'd been taking the bit in his teeth. He smiled wryly. "I guess I've lamed myself like the sorrel."

Trance coiled the whip.

"Back to your work," he ordered the grooms. He smiled understandingly at George. "I was a boy once myself, Master George. Those exciting

times pass by too quickly before one must concern
himself with the serious affairs of men and nations.
Enjoy the stables, Master George."

He strode away. George turned to Sampson.

"You should have insisted on telling me about
the horse."

"Massa George," the trainer gravely reminded
him, "along with this here place, yo' pappy also
left you a temper."

George nodded. "Well, it's under control now.
But too late. I guess I'll be off to school soon."

"Until then," Sampson smiled, "there's a
powerful heap of ridin' can be done!"

"Better riding," said George, laughing. "That
is, if you've still got the patience to help me."

"I'll teach you, Massa George! Yassuh! I'll
make you a better rider than any gentleman in
the Virginia Colony." Sampson's voice rose happily. "Better even than any officer in His Majesty
King George's Army!"

George grinned. "Careful how you talk about
our king, Sampson. I may want a commission in
his army or navy . . . when I come of age."

He forgot his blistered feet as he walked into
the stables with Sampson. It was good to feel relaxed and boyish again. The future master of
Stafford. But more important, the master now of
himself.

Merritt P. Allen

The Mudhen, V. S.

Sitting cross-legged on the grass of the back campus, Froggie Bates looked earnestly at the sky and repeated, " 'Breathes there a man with soul so dead who never to himself hath said—hath said—hath said—' Mud, what was it the guy said to himself?" He appealed to his roommate, known to the whole school as The Mudhen.

"It sounds like a horse," The Mudhen remarked, from his horizontal position on the ground.

"Naw! He didn't say, 'It sounds like a horse.' That doesn't make sense."

"Shut up!" The Mudhen rolled on his side.

"But, Mud, I've got to learn the thing before class tomorrow."

"*It is* a horse. I can hear it walking with my ear to the ground like an Indian."

"What's biting you? A horse walking with his ear to the ground like an Indian!"

"It's in the Bumble Bee's garden." The Mudhen got up with unusual speed. "We'd better see about it in case he is away."

"What harm will he do if he is away?"

"The *horse*, jughead, he'll ruin the garden."

They climbed the fence, edged through some shrubbery, and came upon Mr. Beeman digging in a flower bed. He looked up and smiled in his usual friendly way.

"I thought I heard a horse walking," The Mudhen explained.

"What you heard was probably William Shakespeare," Mr. Beeman answered and went on digging.

"I—" The Mudhen paused and blinked. "I thought it was a horse."

"William seemed restless, so I tethered him behind the barn," Mr. Beeman said casually.

They hardly expected to find the Bard there, but just to put things straight they looked behind the barn. There, walking round and round a picket pin, was a fat little horse that looked lonesome and pricked up his ears with a pleasant expression.

"This is William Shakespeare," said Mr. Beeman, coming around the corner of the barn. "He belongs to my sister, who has left him with me during her vacation."

"Swell! I love horses." The Mudhen went over and stroked William's neck. "Do you object, sir, if I come over and see him once in a while?"

"Assuredly not," Mr. Beeman said eagerly. "You may take full charge of him, if you wish."

"Mud doesn't love him that much," Froggie said.

"Yes, I do too!" The Mudhen declared warmly. "I'll be tickled pink to look after him. Frog, go bring him a pail of water."

"Me!" Froggie snorted. "He's not my baby."

"Run along and get the water—that is, if you want some help with your math tonight," The Mudhen said sweetly.

"You can't kick me around that way!" Froggie cried. "I'll get the water because I like the horse, not because you told me to." He walked away with an independent air.

So began their friendship with William Shakespeare. Why he was so called was never explained to them, nor did it matter. They, like most boys, had a fondness for animals and this one was fat and friendly and something different to play with outside of school. When it came to caring for him, The Mudhen figured out what should be done and Froggie did it, for that was the way their perfect partnership worked. And it was all right with Mr. Beeman, whose interest in horses was nil plus the square of zero multiplied by ten.

It may be that Fate arranged this setup so that when it became necessary for Mr. Beeman to be out of town for a few days the horse would not be neglected. But if Fate left the cover off the grain bin that day, she was either downright careless or hopelessly dumb about the habits of horses. At any rate, William Shakespeare found the box open and ate three times as much grain as he was equipped to handle. When the boys went over to bed him down for the night they found him inflated to blimplike proportions, sweating rivulets, and breathing in a way that brought terror to the hearts of his friends.

"G—G—Gosh sakes! He's g-got the fl-flu," Froggie chattered.

"He's got the bellyache," said the practical Mudhen, pointing at the empty grain bin.

"Is that all?" Froggie looked relieved, for he had suffered that ailment and survived.

"All!" The Mudhen, who knew something about horses, gave him a look. "It's enough to kill him. Beat it to a phone and call a vet."

"But, Mud, they cost four or five bucks."

"That's cheaper than a dead horse. Scram!"

Froggie may have scrammed, but it seemed to the anxious nurse that a fossilized snail could have passed him on the first turn. Minutes masquerading as hours dragged by, while William Shakespeare groaned and sweated and finally lay down broadside on the barn floor. The Mudhen rubbed him with swabs of hay and begged him not to pass out.

"You've got to hang on, Willie," he implored. "If you croak I'll be in dutch with the Bumble Bee and he will be in dutch with his sister. No matter how punk you feel, you mustn't let us down. Please buck up."

But no vet came. Finally Froggie galloped in carrying an old-fashioned dinner horn and a huge pitcher full of liquid.

"Where's the vet?" The Mudhen shouted.

"Sick," Froggie panted.

"There are two in town."

"The other one is away. I called the sick one again and told him it was a matter of life and death, for William Shakespeare has an awful bellyache. He tried to be smart and said the British Museum knows more about Shakespeare than he does, so I'd better call them."

"Didn't you tell him William is a horse?"

"Sure, soon's I got a chance to. He said a name like that was enough to give any horse a bellyache."

"And he isn't coming?"

"I told you, Mud, he's sick—sick in bed. But he said to give him, that is, to give William, a pound of baking soda in two quarts of water and exercise him."

"Exercise him!" The Mudhen gestured toward prostrate William. "How you goin' to exercise a horse that can't walk?"

"How do I know? I'm telling you what the man said. So I got the soda from the Bumble Bee's housekeeper and she found a tin horn for me and—"

"For pete's sake! What are you goin' to do with a tin horn?"

"It's not for tooting," Froggie assured him. "The vet said to pour the dope down William's neck through a funnel, but we couldn't find a funnel so Mrs. Stebbins said to use this horn. We poured some water through it and it perks."

Perking in the kitchen sink was one thing, but perking down the throat of William Shakespeare was something else. Rank amateurs though they were, the boys knew that the horse's powerful teeth could crush a finger like a stick of candy.

"But we've got to give him that medicine,"

The Mudhen said grimly. "Whether he lives or dies we can't have folks sayin' we didn't try to save him."

"If he croaks, the Bears will kid us raw," Froggie prophesied.

The Mudhen nodded, well knowing the heathenish temperament of the rival fraternity.

"There must be a vet in some other town," Froggie reasoned. "I'll go ask the telephone girl to call—"

"Eureka!" The Mudhen interrupted.

"Is that a town or a vet?"

"It's this." The Mudhen dived into a dark corner of the barn and came up with a stick about a foot long with a large hole in the middle. "It's a piece of busted ladder. We'll put it between William's jaws and stick the horn through the hole. If he bites, he'll bite the wood."

"Hot dog!" Froggie's tone paid tribute to genius, "They oughta give you a vet's degree or somethin'—like H.D.—horse doctor."

"Please." The Mudhen closed his eyes in pain. "V.S.—Veterinary Surgeon—not horse doctor."

Deceptively, under pretense of inserting a bit, they persuaded the horse to open his mouth and accept the stick. Gently they worked it back as far as it would go and ever so carefully pushed the dinner horn into the hole, its small end aimed down his gullet. Then, naturally enough, they discovered that while William was in that position nothing would run down his throat. It would be necessary to get him on his feet, pull his head up by running the halter rope through a convenient ring in the ceiling and then, standing on the stairs, transfer the bellywash from the pitcher to the tin horn.

William was, or thought he was, too ill to resist, so eventually he stood with upturned mouth wide open.

"I'll latch onto the halter. You hop up the stairs and drench him," The Mudhen said, with a professional air.

"Do what?" Froggie gasped.

"Drench him. That's what vets call giving a big dose of liquid."

"Drench" was the exact word for it and Froggie was the exact drenchee. William inhaled about a quart of the stuff and then sent it back, propelled by a mighty cough and heave that first drowned Froggie, then knocked him off the stairs. The pitcher did not break because it landed on his stomach and emptied itself down his trousers legs. Intuitively The Mudhen leaped backward and let go the knotted halter rope, which flew up and smashed the electric light bulb.

"Are you hurt, Frog?" The Mudhen shouted.

But before the soggy Froggie could answer, the darkness was rent, shattered, pulverized by a blast of sound.

"Jeeeepers!" The Mudhen reeled backward, overtook the open feed bin, and jackknifed into it. The floor trembled as the ailing William bolted for the door, taking the fiendish noise with him.

"Where are you, Mud?" Froggie sounded terrified.

"Coming out of the feed box. What happened to Shakespeare?"

"I—I guess he exploded. It's all over me."

"But the noise? That was no explosion."

Just then it sounded again outside the barn, a terrific metallic bray that would have raised gooseflesh on a fencepost.

"Jumping bobcats! He's blowing the dinner horn, Frog."

"William Shakespeare?"

"That board with the horn in it must be stuck in his mouth."

"Oh, my gosh! What'll we do, Mud?"

"You mean, what will he do?"

"He's doing it."

He was, with gusto. All his life William had been a well-mannered horse, and it is no disparagement to record that he suddenly abandoned

his former behavior pattern. Why not? In itself a bellyache is hard to endure and when, in addition, one finds one's mouth filled with something that feels like a woodpile and sounds like the Last Trumpet, one is persuaded to get the heck out of there. So he galloped down the driveway and into the street, giving voice to what was probably the first equine horn solo.

Under ordinary conditions a stanch dinner horn of the old school can make itself heard for a mile, but when it is activated by the lung power of a panic-stricken horse its range becomes amazing. And so does its tone, which acquires not only enormous volume but a weird, unearthly note of alarm that might cause a stuffed crocodile to climb a tree. William Shakespeare made the most of his unsought opportunity by putting his four feet to the pavement in a way reminiscent of Paul Revere, or rather of Paul's horse.

Then something else happened. By one of the most remarkable coincidences in modern times, at the very moment of William's setting forth, the main electric line went flooie and the village became dark. And down the black street, hoofs pounding and horn screeching, went William Shakespeare like a messenger of doom.

"Air raid!" someone screamed, and the words took wing. "Air raid! Air raid! Air raid!" flew along streets, across gardens, over housetops. Somewhere someone snatched a phone and called emergency headquarters.

"Can you verify it?" the operator snapped.

"Don't stand there arguing. They've landed by parachute outside town. Grabbed all the cars, cut the wires, but a guy on horseback got through. Blow, you fool!"

The operator was still hesitating when a clatter of hoofs and a wild blast of alarm drew near and passed into the darkness. "That guy is a hero," the girl sobbed and threw the siren switch.

"Oh, my gosh!" Froggie caught hold of The Mudhen as the wail rose to high heaven. "They'll put us in the pedal fenitentiary for this!"

"Come on!" The Mudhen tugged at him. "We've got to hide that horse before the lights come on."

"You're nuts."

"Everybody is. Scram!"

They ran down the street, that was intermittently lighted by passing cars. By then police sirens were adding to the din and some misguided patriot was clanging a church bell like mad.

"I can't hear William any more," Froggie panted. "We're stuck."

The Mudhen stopped abruptly and pulled his partner onto a lawn.

"You know something, Frog?"

"Not a thing," Froggie admitted cheerfully.

"If that horse has any sense he'll beat it home where the Bumble Bee's sister lives. That's just outside of town. Let's go."

"There'll be nobody there. She's gone visiting."

"We don't want anybody there except William. Come on! We'll cut through this garden to the back street."

A truck backfired a few feet away and from a window above them a woman shrieked, "That was a bomb! Get ready to jump!"

"Follow me, Frog," The Mudhen shouted.

"I can't see where—" Froggie's voice stopped with a smothered squawk.

"What the heck!" The Mudhen turned back. "What's wrong, Frog?"

"They dropped a parachute on me!" Froggie sounded underground. "Pull it off me, Mud, I'm smothering!"

The Mudhen groped until he found cloth, yards of it, a great blob that seemed to cover the whole lawn. It was heaving violently and from its depths came muffled cries and grunts. There was a sudden ripping sound and Froggie began to cough and sputter like a stalling motor. The Mudhen put out his hands and found the air full of soft floating, flakelike things.

"Feathers!" he cried, enlightened. "Somebody dropped a feather bed on you. Hey, you up there! Don't throw anything more down."

"I'm going to jump on the bed before the house burns down," the upstairs lady shrieked, as the old truck backfired again in the dark street. "They're bombing us!"

"Don't jump!" The Mudhen yelled. "There's no fire."

She caught the word "fire" and flung it around for all she was worth: "Fire! Fire! Fire!"

"I'll send in an alarm," a neighbor whooped.

"I've got my own hose hooked up," said a voice nearby.

There was a gurgle and a hiss as a vicious unseen stream of water hurtled through the night.

"Aoooow!" Froggie's voice rose and fell with a splash.

"Shut it off, you sap!" The Mudhen roared.

"I'll keep things wet," the man promised heroically.

He did, very wet, so wet that by the time the boys were out of range they made a piker of the proverbial drowned rat.

"Pft! Pft!" Froggie said.

"What ails you?" The Mudhen asked testily.

"You'd spit if you were plastered a foot thick

with wet feathers."

"Snap out of it. We've got to find that horse."

"I hope he's dead."

"I don't. I'm responsible for him."

"Then you're responsible for all this mess."

"Shut up!"

They listened for a while to the wild sounds in the village, of which William Shakespeare and his horn were no longer audible parts. It was possible, as The Mudhen had suggested, that he had fled to his old home. Acting on that hunch, they made their way there and found him peacefully eating grass behind the empty house. Somewhere along the way he had lost his noisemaking apparatus and also his bellyache. Stealthily, they tied him in an open shed and went back to the school, where their absence had not been noticed.

They spent the next day looking innocent and listening hard to various wild speculations as to what had caused last night's false alarms, but heard no word to indicate that the town guessed what it owed William. That evening, by devious back streets, they escorted him to Mr. Beeman's barn and left him to his hay.

A few days later Mr. Beeman came home and hailed the passing Mudhen.

"I chanced to meet the veterinarian this morning," he said. "He told me you phoned him that William was ill while I was away."

"Yes, sir. The vet knows his stuff. He said exercise would be good for William and it cured him."

"Thank you so much. But I regret causing you so much bother."

"Don't mention it, sir." The Mudhen gazed thoughtfully at the sky. "It wasn't the least bit of bother to anyone."

Joseph Stocker

Horse With Cow Savvy

The bay stallion bore an impressive-sounding name—Steel Dust. But he wasn't overly prepossessing in appearance. He lacked the slim, whippetlike form of the distance racer. Instead he had the stocky, muscular build of the Virginia short horse or quarter horse, so-called because this breed was fastest at short distances—a quarter-mile or less. Also he was twelve years old, which, in a horse, is getting on toward middle age. Besides all that he had an oddly sleepy look about him that elicited amiable jibes from bystanders as his owners Mid Perry and Jones Greene led him toward the starting post.

"Ya reckon that horse'll stay awake long enough ta race?" called one.

"Maybe he oughta have a little nap first, huh?" spoke up another.

Perry and Greene only grinned. Steel Dust, they figured, could speak for himself when the time came.

It was a brisk spring Sunday in 1855. The little Texas frontier town of McKinney was a-jam with people, come from all over that county and several neighboring counties to see the big event—a match race between Steel Dust and Monmouth. Monmouth was the younger of the two, a Kentucky short horse owned by one Harrison Stiff. Like Perry and Greene, Stiff was a settler who'd emigrated from the East. And, like Steel Dust, Monmouth was a mighty fast horse—faster, folks were saying, than a rush telegram traveling on a downhill wire. Just as Steel Dust was mopping up everything in sight at quarter-mile races, so was Monmouth, until there was only one thing left to do: Match the two of them together and see which was the fastest horse in those parts.

Steel Dust's jockey was a young Negro named Tom McKnight, who weighed so little that he had to smear molasses all over the horse's back and sides in order to stick on. The name of Monmouth's rider has been lost in the shuffle of history. But not the results of the race. Steel Dust, as he stood at the starting post, still had that sleepy look. However, if anyone had bet against him on the strength of it, it would have been the deception of the year, because when the gun went off, Steel Dust leaped away as if shot out of a cannon. Monmouth got away fast, too. But he was still a head behind Steel Dust at the start, and a half-length behind him at the midpoint, and a full length and a half behind when they flashed past the quarter-mile finish line.

The spectacular match race held that spring Sunday at McKinney, Texas, accomplished two things: It made Steel Dust the most celebrated horse of the frontier. And it demonstrated, if demonstration were needed, that the quarter horse had won a secure place in the life of the West and the esteem of western men.

The passing of time and the coming of the automobile and the truck haven't altered that fact. The quarter horse is as indispensable in the West, and wherever else cattle are raised, as he was a hundred years ago. You can't cut a cow out of a herd with a Ford two-door, and chasing a dogie in a Chevrolet pickup would be pretty unwieldy. It still takes a horse to do those chores. Moreover, it takes a horse that has what ranchers call "cow savvy"—a horse that's stocky, powerful, gentle, and smart, that can start up like a jackrabbit and whirl on a manhole cover—a horse that can be worked or raced or ridden for pleasure. And all of that spells quarter horse.

This versatile animal traces his history back earlier even than that other famous breed, the Thoroughbred—back to the colonial days in tidewater Virginia. Then, as now, he was what is known as a "using" horse. The colonists worked him weekdays, raced him Sundays, and bred fastest to fastest. For their races they measured off a quarter-mile section of country road or village dirt street. If they lacked money, which they usually did, they bet saddles or bridles or even a crop against a crop. And they called that good-natured all-round horse of theirs a "quarter-of-a-mile running horse," which in time got shortened to quarter horse.

As the frontier moved west, so did he. He carried Sam Houston into Texas and he was with Davy Crockett at the Alamo and with Custer at the Little Big Horn. He helped plow the black earth of Texas and round up cattle in New Mexico. And between times he carried kids to school and brought guests to the ranch for the wedding of the rancher's daughter to the boy from the next county.

When some one stallion stood out from the rest, he was greatly in demand for breeding—to sire colts and thus pass along a bloodline that was considered something special. Steel Dust sired so many that he almost created a "breed within a breed," as the saying went. In fact, for years quarter horses were as often called "Steel Dusts." Even now Steel Dust blood is claimed for so many quarter horses that, if all the claims were true, there'd be Steel Dusts overflowing both ends of the country and spilling into the oceans.

Many a quarter horse, however, has shown his spunk or made his mark in the world of horsedom and done it with not a single drop of Steel Dust blood in his veins.

The story of Joe Reed II exemplifies the sort of thing I have in mind.

Joe was a quarter horse stallion belonging to an Arizona cowpuncher named Bert Wood. He was just a working cowboy's horse, with no special training for the track. But Wood thought he saw greatness in the stallion and longed to race him.

The chances that Joe Reed II would ever distinguish himself on the track were pretty slim, though, Wood had to admit. He was seven years old, which is old for a racehorse. And he had a bad left foreleg. When he was a colt, running free on the range, he'd skidded into a barbwire fence and come away with a deep cut. The leg was still a bit enlarged and had a way of being somewhat stiff until it warmed up.

As if this weren't bad enough, something else happened just a few days before Joe was to run his first race at a track in Tucson. Wood was riding him up a dry wash, in pursuit of a cow, when Joe stepped on a piece of broken bottle and cut his foot badly. Wood gave some thought to canceling out Joe's scheduled appearance at Tucson. Then he decided, for no really good reason except a hunch, to go ahead.

That first race was on a Sunday. When Joe Reed II limped past the judges' stand toward the starting gate, somebody down by the fence could be heard saying scornfully, "Why, that old horse won't stand a chance," which certainly seemed the safest prediction of the day. After all, a seven-year-old horse, without racing experience or training—and crippled to boot!

Joe was running in a field of six, and all five of the others got away before Joe did and were several lengths ahead of him when he turned on the juice. He whipped past them as though they had buckets on their feet and beat the next best across the finish line by a half-length.

A week later Bert Wood ran him again, against competition that was amongst the best to be found at any of the quarter-horse tracks. During the intervening week, because of his lame foot, Joe Reed II hadn't even been out of his stall. But he beat the field by two full lengths.

Just one week after that Joe ran his third and

last race. Again because of the foot, he hadn't been out of his stall. And again the field included some of the nation's fastest quarter horses, one of them being Clabber, a world's champion.

Joe and Clabber broke away from the starting gate simultaneously. But as they came out, Clabber veered into Joe Reed II. It was no fault of his jockey. It just happened, and Joe almost stumbled off the track.

Then he regained his stride. He caught up with Clabber, and the two horses, outdistancing the rest of the field, pounded neck and neck down the straightaway. When they flashed across the finish line, it looked like an absolute tie. But the official photographs showed Joe Reed II to be a half a head in front. And something else was discovered. Joe had run that race with blood spurting from his injured foot every bit of the way.

Now please don't take from all this the notion that quarter horses are mainly race horses. They're not. They're mainly work horses for farm and ranch, not only in the West but all over the country. And they're "fun" horses, for riding out across rolling hills on a balmy Saturday afternoon, and for sitting tall and proud in the saddle as you ride through canyons of people in a rodeo parade. Only incidentally are they race horses, although quarter-horse racing is getting bigger all the time.

A good many western cities now have quarter-horse tracks, and prices up to $125,000 are being paid for the top runners.

Where the quarter horse really shines, though, is as a cowboy's horse—as a cutting horse or roping horse. And that sort of thing takes tough and skillful men and tough and maneuverable horses.

Watch closely from the top of a nearby fence while a cutting horse is at work, for instance, and you'll understand what ranchers mean when they talk about a quarter horse having "cow savvy."

The ancient art of cutting dates back to the days of the unfenced range. Periodically all the cattle belonging to several ranchers in a neighborhood would be rounded up on a stretch of open country. Then the cowboys from the various spreads would go in on horseback and "cut out" their cattle from the common herd. The cutting horse had to be able to work efficiently and quietly. He had to cut out one cow after another, keep them from rejoining the herd (which cows are forever bent on doing) and, through it all, take pains not to "spook" the herd. He had to be fast of mind and fast on his feet, able to whirl like a ballet dancer, stop on a poker chip, and keep two thoughts ahead of the critter he was cutting. "I've seen a cutting horse down in some awful positions—almost down on the ground, spread out like an ink blotter," said an old-time cowman. "But it wouldn't make any difference which way the cow went—she was looking right square in that horse's eye when she stopped."

The era of the open range is long gone, but the cutting horse still has his work to do. He cuts steers out of a herd to be branded or doctored or sent to market. And the requirements are the same as they've always been: Cut 'em out. Keep 'em out. Don't "spook" the herd. And don't run 'em farther than necessary. Cowmen are in the business of putting beef on cattle, not giving them reducing exercises.

Like so many other aspects of ranch life, the art of cutting has moved from the corral to the competitive arena. Cutting-horse competition is one of the big attractions in the cattle country. And the prize money reaches respectable proportions, as do the prices being paid for top cutting horses— $30,000 and up.

In the arena, the cutting horse and his rider have certain rules to abide by. There's a bunch of cattle at one end of the arena. Horse and rider have two and one-half minutes to go in and cut out as many as they can. What makes it tough is that there are two "hazers" in the arena whose job is to yell and flap their arms and try to chase

the poor, confused calves back into the herd as
fast as they're cut out of it. If the "hazers" suc-
ceed—if a calf manages to slither past your horse
and rejoin the herd—you're docked so many
points. It's a merry and furious game of wits and
reflexes, of darting and dodging and wheeling.

A good cutting horse can cut out three cows
from a herd, and keep them cut out, in two and
one-half minutes. And he does it pretty much on
his own. All you do is ride into the herd, indicate
the animal you want cut out, and drop the reins.
Your horse takes it from there. When you want
him to stop what he's doing and go in after another calf, you pull on the reins and touch his
neck. All in all, cutting-horse competition de-
mands more brains and stamina of a horse than
almost any other skill.

It's those two things—brains and stamina—
that make the quarter horse an invaluable and
almost indestructible tool of the rancher's trade.
And they've even been known to make him a
hero, which is as good a way as any of leading up
to what happened in the case of Billy Webb and
Blackhawk.

Billy was the fourteen-year-old son of a Colorado rancher. Blackhawk was his horse. Well,
not actually his, although it amounted to that.
Blackhawk was one of a dozen or so quarter

horses on the Webb ranch. But Billy rode him most of the time and even gave him his name, which was fitting enough, considering that Blackhawk was a glossy jet black except for a small white blaze on his forehead.

It was on a late summer day that the thing happened. Billy had ridden Blackhawk out from the ranch several miles to help his father and his father's cowhands hunt for a missing steer. Quite suddenly, as those things have a way of doing along about that time of year in Colorado, a cloudburst struck. Then, to make matters worse, and just as Billy was turning Blackhawk homeward in the pelting rain, he felt a pain in his stomach that was like a hot knife stabbing into him. What he had no way of knowing was that he'd suffered an acute attack of appendicitis.

Doubled over from the pain of it, blinded by the rain and wind, he could do nothing except give Blackhawk his head and hang on as best he could. And in that fashion they set off for home.

Between them and the ranch lay a creek. In normal weather it was a well-behaved little stream that could be forded in a few steps and a splash or two. But now it was a swift, churning torrent of dirty, silt-laden water. When Blackhawk reached the water's edge, he stopped. Billy, thinking they could still ford the creek, tried to urge him in. Blackhawk balked. Billy, grimacing with the pain that the effort cost him, slapped the horse's streaming flanks with his heels. Still Blackhawk refused to move, some instinct apparently warning him that he would be swept off his feet in the raging water if he tried to cross.

The boy could think of only one other possibility. Close by, dimly visible through the driving rain, was a railroad trestle. Billy doubted that a horse which couldn't be persuaded to ford a stream could be persuaded to walk across a trestle with slippery ties a foot apart. But he had to try.

To his surprise, Blackhawk hesitated only a second. Then he started across the trestle. Head down, his muscles quivering so that Billy could feel them between his legs, Blackhawk took one slow and cautious step after another.

Billy Webb, staring down between the ties at the tumbling brown waters beneath, knew how great was the danger. If Blackhawk lost his footing and fell, Billy would be thrown into the stream, and, helpless as he was from the massive pain in his belly, he would be unable to swim ashore.

Once Blackhawk did slip. They were just past the halfway point, and the horse's right front hoof suddenly slid off into space. Billy's heart almost stopped beating. But the horse managed to keep his other three hoofs firmly planted and, with gingerly care, pulled his right front foot into place on one of the ties.

Then they were off the trestle and on safe ground. Ten minutes later they were at the ranch house. And ten minutes after that Billy's father was bundling the pain-crumpled boy into a pickup truck for a dash through the storm to the nearest town and a doctor. He underwent an immediate operation and came through it in fine shape, although the doctor said that if there'd been much more delay, he might not have survived. Billy and his family were grateful to the doctor and to medical science. But they knew that the credit for saving his life had to be shared equally with a horse—a brainy, gutty, little black quarter horse with a white blaze on his forehead.

I heard the story of Billy Webb and Blackhawk from a cowboy I met at a Colorado rodeo. He happened to have been working on the Webb ranch at the time the incident occurred.

We were standing beside one of the chutes while we talked, and as he finished the story, my cowboy friend lifted his big hat and smoothed back his hair with the palm of his hand and lowered his hat again.

"The way I figure it," he said, squinting thoughtfully, "they just don't come much smarter or spunkier than those there quarter horses."

And that's about the way I figure it, too.

Carl Henry Rathjen

Sacrifice Spurs

Dave Remy spotted the silver spurs in a Sacramento store window that California dawn of February 23, 1855, as he and old Jep Frey, his dad's ranch foreman, hurried down crowded K Street.

"Jep, look!" He pointed as gold miners and townspeople jostled by on their way to the riverfront. Jep Frey turned his gray head from the street jammed with stagecoaches awaiting the arrival of the steamboat from Frisco.

"Think you've earned them?" he asked.

Dave tugged his gaze from the spurs. Beauties. Just the kind that his dad, recovering from a horse's kick, had said he could buy if he proved himself man enough to get a good price for cattle in Sacramento.

"Yesterday," Dave began defensively, "you

said that $12,500 in gold wasn't bad at all in these hard times."

Then he saw the twinkle in Jep's eyes. He started eagerly toward the store, but Jep grabbed his arm.

"You can buy spurs any time. It ain't every day we get to town to see the steamboat arrive from the big city. And look at all them stage-coaches waitin' to gallop to Hangtown, Auburn, Marysville, everywhere in the Mother Lode Country."

"You look," said Dave, his excited eyes on those spurs again. "I'll find you down on the levee."

But Jep hung onto his arm as the crowd shouldered by.

"Better give me that deposit certificate, son. Your pa's countin' heavy on that gold. And this is the kind of a crowd that pickpockets like."

The word "son" stung a bit. Dave spoke up.

"I was old enough to sell those cattle, Jep. Guess I'm man enough to take care of that gold certificate—and this, too." Dave patted the bulge of his wallet which had the five hundred dollars his father had said to bring home. "Besides, the certificate can't be cashed by anyone except me or Dad. His gold is safe in the bank."

Jep studied him, then smiled.

"See you down at the levee then—man-size spurs and all."

Dave dashed into the store. He strapped on the silver spurs, though it would be a few hours before he, Jep, and the ranchhands got their horses from the livery stable and started home. As he proudly jingled out on K Street again, a boisterous group of miners jostled him. He quickly felt for the wallet's reassuring bulge.

He thought of Jep's warning. He'd heard stories too about pickpocketing. The hard times tempted people to be lightfingered. Gold miners were up against it because this winter's scant rainfall had shut down placer operations. As a result, San Francisco business slumped. The East had had a hard winter too. So had his dad. But that gold deposit certificate was a windfall that would hold things together.

Dave suddenly didn't like the idea of getting into the thick of the riverfront crowd to look for Jep. Someone, smart enough to steal that certificate from him, might be clever enough to get it honored at the bank. His dad would surely lose the ranch then. So, reluctantly turning his back on the arriving steamboat, he strolled up K Street like a man too busy and important to be interested in ordinary excitements—until he reached Bremond's restaurant. Hey, he hadn't had breakfast yet!

Gravely, as befitted a man who had earned his spurs and would some day own one of the largest ranches in the Sacramento Valley, he entered and ordered—two stacks of flap-jacks with sausages, a side order of bacon and eggs, fresh rolls and jam, coffee, two wedges of pie and a bottle of root juice.

With that man-sized meal straining his belt, he jingled outside. Everyone was now hurrying from the riverfront toward a crowd farther uptown. Dave wondered what the new excitement was about. Then hard fingers bit into his arm. Jep Frey glared hard at him.

"Where in blazes have you been? I've looked all over for you! What're you doing *standing* here?"

"I've been having breakfast," Dave began, puzzled.

"Spurs! Breakfast!" snapped Jep Frey. "Ain't you heard there's a run on the bank before it closes its doors?"

"The Adams Bank?" Dave gasped.

"What else would I be worried about?" Jep retorted, yanking him out of his daze. "If you'd been at the levee, you'd have heard that the panic from the East hit Frisco yesterday. It started a run—everybody runnin' to the bank, all at the same time, and drawin' out their money. All the Frisco banks are closed. The Adams home office there has failed, closed forever. And it's anybody's guess how long the Sacramento branch can stay open and pay out—"

Dave heard no more as he dashed ahead. His dad, the ranch, everything depended on that $12,000 gold deposit. With Jep shoving behind him, he fought through the crowd into the bank. He thrust the deposit certificate at a harried clerk, caught at the lapels by Jep's big fist.

"I can't!" yelled the clerk. "Wait your turn in line!"

The crowd agreed angrily. A miner called to Dave.

"You should have got here half an hour ago, kid."

A half-hour ago he'd been swaggering his new spurs into Bremond's. Dave couldn't look at Jep as they sought the end of the line. Outside. Down the street. Around the corner. Endless. Dave's heart sank clear down to those danged spurs.

"We'll be all day reaching the window," he groaned.

"If the bank's got any money or gold left by then," Jep glowered.

Dave felt like giving up that man-sized break-fast. He stared at the certificate, now just an empty promise to pay . . .

"Jep! I've still got a chance! This is payable at any branch of the Adams bank. There won't be a run like this in Hangtown, Auburn, anywhere in the Mother Lode Country. Not yet anyway."

"The telegraph already flashed the bad news from here all over California," Jep growled. "Wait a minute!" he squinted. "There's not a chance in California. But, Dave, there isn't any telegraph line to Portland, Oregon! They won't know up there! So if we catch the ship Columbia sailing from Frisco this afternoon—"

Dave turned eagerly toward the river front.

"That wad of five hundred will take care of our passage," he agreed, patting his wallet. Then he stopped short, "Jep! The Columbia will carry the bad news *with* us! And the Portland branch will refuse to honor the certificate when they hear how everything's closed down here!"

Jep looked suddenly haggard, then spoke through his teeth.

"I hope you're satisfied with the price you paid for those spurs. Twelve thousand in gold *and* your dad's ranch!"

Dave blinked down at the silver spurs. Sacrifice

spurs! They'd made him feel so grownup, ready to take his place beside his father riding about the ranch. Riding . . .

"Jep, these spurs may save everything yet."

Jep laughed harshly.

"If you mean what I think—"

"I'll beat the Columbia by *riding* to Portland."

"You're crazy!" Jep exploded. "It's seven hundred miles!"

"You've called me a riding fool," Dave argued. "You've taught me how to ride, toughened me up."

"Not for seven hundred miles over mountains against time. You'd have to ride day and night for a week . . . *if* you could stay in the saddle that long—"

"I've got to," Dave cut in. "It's my only chance."

"It's throwin' the chance away! Take the Columbia, son. When she docks in Portland, we'll get to the bank ahead of the bad news and—"

"It'll be shouted ashore before we can get off her," Dave insisted. "Then what?"

"It's a better try than having you fold up somewhere in the mountains. You ain't made of iron. Gimme that deposit certificate. *I'm* takin' the Columbia!"

They turned as a steamboat whistle sounded. Then Dave raced for the riverfront. Jep panted after him.

"Now, you're showin' sense, son. We'll—"

Dave sprinted as he saw a sternwheeler edging away from the wharf. Jep followed behind him.

"Not that boat, you fool! She's goin' upriver!"

Dave leaped wildly across water. His spurs gouged planking as a deckhand caught him. He turned quickly and called to Jep on the receding wharf:

"I know it—I'll be waiting with the gold when the Columbia docks in Portland."

Jep gave him a hard look, then vanished into the crowd.

Dave paced as the sternwheeler thrashed its tortuous way up the Sacramento River. What had he jumped into with those blamed spurs? Seven hundred hard-riding miles. But the more he thought about his pop's losing the ranch, the more he knew he had made the only possible decision. Get to Portland *before*, not with, the bad news. He prayed that the Columbia was as slow as this creaking riverboat.

At last the old tub swung into Knight's Landing, forty-two miles upriver from Sacramento. Dave jumped to the wharf and cut short the greeting from old man Knight, his father's friend.

"I need a good *fast* horse, Mr. Knight. Will you sell me one?"

"You can't buy a horse from me, son." Dave turned away angrily. A fine friend! "But take my best mount at the head of the wharf."

"Thanks," Dave grinned over his shoulder. Excited, he startled the drowsing bay stallion. It reared into life, fighting his efforts to mount. Swinging up, he pricked it with a spur. The lunging stallion nearly threw him. His cheeks burned as everyone stared. Nice way to start the long ride to Portland, forgetting all the horsemanship Jep had taught him!

He calmed himself, then the horse, walking it a quarter-mile till it became accustomed to his weight. Then a quarter-mile of trotting. Another galloping. Trot again. Walk. Trot. Gallop again with the other forefoot leading this time. Give the horse a chance to stay fresh longer, keep from getting leg-weary.

Riding north through the hot, dry Sacramento Valley he glanced eastward toward the High Sierra draped with snow. Their ranch nestled over there in the foothills, its entire future dependent on a nest-egg of gold in Portland, nearly seven hundred miles away. Dave tugged down his hat brim as he spurred the stallion ahead.

Late that afternoon he rode the weary horse up to a ranchhouse huddling under towering eucalyptus trees. A young man and a woman, holding a baby, came out as he dismounted patting the stallion.

"Sir," Dave requested, "will you sell me a horse and return this one to Mr. Knight down the valley?"

"Reckon I can," said the man. "But if you've ridden all the way from Knight's you'd better set awhile."

"Just in time for supper," smiled the young woman. Dave realized he hadn't eaten all day . . . not since Bremond's!

"Thanks, but I haven't the time. Now about a horse, sir."

After he saddled up while explaining his haste, the young woman handed him a package of food to take along.

"I'll pray that you make it to Portland in time," she said. As he rode away, he heard her speak to her husband. "I used to envy people who had money in the bank."

He traveled fast until darkness blotted out everything but the stars. He let the horse have its head and kept his eye on the north star . . . until it exploded into a thousand stars when the limb of a tree smashed him in the face. He clung to the saddle, fighting dizziness. He ought to wait for daylight to travel in this strange country. But the Columbia would steam north all night. He squinted into the darkness and urged the horse onward.

At dawn he roused a fat, grumpy liveryman in Red Bluff and made a deal to trade horses. Asking the man to call him in an hour, he burrowed into a pile of hay. He dreamed he was crawling toward a pile of gold, but someone hauled him back by the shoulder. He fought desperately.

"Easy, kid," a voice said. He opened his eyes to see the liveryman bending over him. "Hour's up," the man grinned.

Dave stumbled to his horse, put his foot in the stirrup, and felt no bulge in his hip pocket. He whirled.

"Where's my wallet?" he demanded, advancing. The man's hand dropped toward a gun. Dave dove, clamping on the wrist. The heavy liveryman swung him off his feet and piled onto him. Dave felt himself being pinned down. He got a leg clear, lifted it, then brought it down hard, driving a silver spur into the man's rump. The liveryman howled. Dave wriggled free, smashed him in the face and got the gun.

"All right, all right," the man yelled. "Here!"

Dave quickly checked the wad in his wallet and, most important of all, the deposit certificate. Mounting, he tossed the gun in the hayloft and rode away.

The sun climbed to the noon sky and hurled its heat into the Sacramento Valley. Mountains shimmered. Dust devils swirled. Dave's eyes smarted with sweat. Twenty-four hours since he'd left Knight's Landing. It seemed like twenty-four years. But here he was, still in this blasted valley, still in California. And the livery stable plug lathering out under him. How had he ever imagined he could make it to Portland in time to save his dad's ranch.

He goaded the wheezing nag to a ranch just south of Redding and bought a chunky pinto which the foreman said would "take the mountains ahead like they was the flats." That night, in black mountains hulking below snow-capped Mt. Shasta, he wished he had bought a coat along with the pinto. The moon hung like ice among brittle stars. Trees cracked in the sharp coldness. He ran beside his trotting horse in an effort to warm up. Back in the saddle he fought drowsiness.

He woke up, half-frozen, outside a cabin above a rushing river as a little gray-headed lady tried to get him out of the saddle. He tumbled off numbly and she steadied him into a kitchen warm with the odor of freshly baked bread. As he thawed out by the stove, he glanced out the window down toward the river where two men, probably her husband and son, were fishing. He shivered.

"W-what r-river is th-that?"

"The Sacramento, son."

He groaned. Just how long was that river? Was he ever going to get out of California and into Oregon? He asked about getting a horse.

"We'll talk about that later," she said, giving him a motherly smile. "You have some breakfast first, and then some rest. You're all tuckered out."

"I had my sleep on the horse," Dave replied, still shivering and trying not to think about a soft bed and warm blankets. She persisted, but tired as he was he wouldn't give in. Too risky. She was a nice old lady who'd think she was doing him a favor to let him sleep on and on and on—while somewhere off the coast the Columbia steamed northward for Portland.

"Then at least," she sighed finally, "you'll let me fix you a man-sized breakfast."

The cool mountains made for fast riding all that day. By nightfall he'd dropped into the valley north of Weed and hoped to keep up the good pace in flat country. Then wind blasted out of the darkness. The notorious wind of that area that could rip a farmer's seed out of the soil. Wind that could almost lift a man from the saddle and tear him away from a desperately needed crop of gold waiting in Portland. A wind that kept him continually battling the horse which wanted to turn tail and drift in the wrong direction.

Feeling battered and beaten from the blustering night, he rode on, and along toward noon of that third day he swayed into Yreka, still in California, but only twenty miles south of the Oregon border. He wanted to keep pushing, but what if he fell asleep in the saddle again and became lost in the mountains? He'd been lucky last night. So, after trading horses and ordering the new one to be saddled and ready to go in an hour, he reluctantly got a room in a hotel.

The bored desk clerk nodded vaguely when Dave asked to be called later. He'd better wake himself up. But how? He was so exhausted he'd fall in too deep for his inner senses to pull him out before precious time had been lost.

He stared about the shabby room. A decrepit bed. A rickety chair. The usual pitcher of water and basin. Battered bureau with cracked mirror. A candle in a bottle. Yawning, he saw the cord from the window shade. An inch or so from the top of the candle he cut a notch clear into the wick. Fastening the cord to the mirror, he strung it through the notch, touching the wick, and tied the other end to the handle of the pitcher balanced precariously on the edge of the bureau and only prevented from tipping by the cord.

Lighting the candle, he spread blankets and pillow on the floor below the bureau and plunged into darkness . . .

. . . until the candle flame burnt down to the cord and severed it. A flood of water doused his head. The pitcher bounced off his chest. He sat up sputtering and reached for his boots . . . and those silver spurs.

North of Yreka the road climbed higher and higher into the Siskiyou Mountains, while the sun dropped lower and lower. In the evening hush of the darkening mountains he was giving his horse a walking breather when he heard hoofs furiously pounding back around the last bend. At least a dozen or more horses. He frowned uneasily. Outlaws? A posse? A bunch out for a hilarious time? He couldn't mix in anything that might delay him.

He spurred into a shadowy clump of brush a moment before a sheriff's posse rounded the bend.

As they charged by the sheriff raised his arm. They hauled horses back on haunches just up the road.

"Don't see his tracks no more, boys. Head back an' watch for where he turned off, th' danged horse thief."

Dave scowled, sliding his hand forward to his horse's nose to prevent it from whinnying. He remembered the shifty-eyed individual who'd traded him this horse, and got the better of the deal at that. He should have obeyed his warning hunches, but he'd been too anxious to get a fresh horse and keep going. Now he was riding a stolen horse, had been spotted on it, and the sheriff was after him!

If he rode out and tried to explain matters, it would mean hours of delay for a checkup. And another thing—frequently "hoss thieves" got no opportunity to alibi! Dave's throat felt dry and tight as the posse rode slowly back in the deepening darkness peering at the ground.

They missed the spot where he'd turned off. Dave sighed through clenched teeth. He'd wait quietly a few moments and then . . . Then he saw a deputy wheeling back for another look!

No chance of explanation now after hiding out. Dave drove his spurs home. His startled horse leaped out, hoofs clawing the road. The posse shouted. Dave streaked around a bend in the road. A long straightaway. He spurred desperately for the next curve as guns barked behind him.

The chase went on and on, neither gaining nor losing as bullets whined past in the straightaways. Sweeping into another straight stretch Dave, bending low in the saddle, saw a blur of white in the darkness ahead. A roadside marker. The Oregon border. The sheriff's authority would cease beyond that. But sometimes sheriffs ignored little legal points!

Dave spurred and lashed. His horse flattened its ears and streaked ahead. Guns blazed in the night behind him. His horse staggered, then pitched him past the marker. Dave rolled limply until his momentum slowed, then gained his feet and raced into the Oregon brush.

"Too late, men," the sheriff called out. "He's across."

"To heck with the line!" a voice retorted. "We've got him now! Laws ain't made for horse thieves!"

Despite the sheriff's commands a lone horseman rode into the brush. Dave crouched in the shadows. Horseless. Hunted. How would he ever get to Portland in time now, if at all? The rider searched closer, his six-shooter glinting in starlight. As he was about to discover Dave, Dave shoved up on the man's boot with all his strength, toppling him from the saddle. Dave grabbed the saddle horn and swung up as the horse darted ahead in panic. Off in the darkness he reined in and shouted back.

"Sheriff, I'm Dave Remy from the Circle R down in the Sacramento Valley. I didn't steal that dead horse. And I'm just *borrowing* this one. I'll send it back."

He rode into the night. Into Oregon. On his way again to Portland. A long, long way yet. But still on his way.

At Hungry Creek he met a man who was returning to California on a borrowed sorrel. They swapped horses and Dave rode the sorrel to its home corral at Bear Creek. On to Jacksonville for an hour's sleep and a fresh horse. Another night of walking, trotting, galloping. He ate, slept, lived in the saddle on long-legged easy-gaited horses, chunky pounders, strawberry roans, chestnuts, bays, pintos. Trading a tired horse for a frisky one. Paying some extra cash if he had to. Anything to keep going.

The morning of the fifth day he fell out of the saddle in the little town of Eugene, Oregon. But an hour later he hauled himself onto a new horse. That night he couldn't keep his bloodshot eyes

focused. His head bobbed and rolled as though on a swivel. He was too weary to run beside the horse to keep himself awake. Riding at a mad gallop to blow away the cobwebs and pound himself awake, he wrote out the horse ahead of schedule.

"How far to Portland?" he murmured, blinking wearily at an innkeeper in French Prairie six mornings after he'd bought the silver spurs.

"Half a day's ride. But you ain't for it, son. Bet your eyes would burn holes in a pillow."

"Not now," Dave snapped. "Get me the fastest horse in town."

He'd have to push and get to the bank before it closed for the day. It wouldn't be open tomorrow if the Columbia had arrived in the meantime. Suppose she'd already made port? What would he do then?

At ten-thirty that morning he spurred his lathered mount to an auctioneer's corral in Oregon City, his eyes feverishly selecting a horse. And at noon he tossed that horse's bridle reins to a boy on the south bank of the Willamette River.

"Ferry to Portland, mister?" another boy called, standing expectantly by a rowboat. Dave shoved it into the river.

"Five dollars if you get me across fast." He squinted toward boats moored on the far side. "The Columbia in from Frisco yet?"

"No, sir. Ain't heard the cannon announcin' that she's comin' up the river."

Dave smiled triumphantly and relaxed a bit. The hot sun, the glinting water, the rhythmic creak of the oarlocks made him sleepy, terribly sleepy. He fought to keep his bloodshot eyes open just a little longer. He doused handfuls of water in his face, over his head. Blam! The cannon! He forgot sleep.

"Ten dollars more, kid, if—"

He grabbed the gunwales as the boy stood back mightily on the oars and nearly toppled him overboard.

"Golly, fifteen dollars!" the kid grunted. "That's more'n dad makes in a week. He'll think I'm a real man."

Dave stared at his spurs.

"Don't get cocky with a pair of silver oars," he muttered. "You might have to make a long hard row with them."

"Huh?"

"Keep rowing," Dave growled, glancing worriedly downriver.

He ran through the streets of Portland, but made himself *walk* into the Adams office, spurs jingling.

"The cashier's out to lunch," a young clerk began doubtfully.

"Where?" Dave demanded. A new voice spoke behind him.

"Something I can do for you?"

Dave handed the deposit certificate to a portly gentleman mouthing a gold toothpick.

"Have you any identification?" the cashier inquired, curiously studying Dave's travel-stained, tousled, bloodshot appearance. He leisurely verified the validity of the certificate, but then suspiciously looked Dave over again.

"Everything seems in order," he said slowly and pointed the toothpick at the certificate. "But there's something odd here. This deposit was made only six days ago down in Sacramento. And the Columbia isn't in yet."

"I rode here. Yes, all seven hundred miles," Dave explained, then went on quickly. "I have important business here, but I *missed* catching the Columbia. It wouldn't have been safe to carry that amount of gold overland with me."

"Quite true," the cashier admitted, but still he hesitated. Dave heard a horse galloping up the street. If he let this pompous bank official stall much longer . . .

"What's wrong with this office?" he snapped. "Haven't you got the gold to—"

"Of course, of course," the man interrupted,

smiling reassuringly at eavesdropping customers. The galloping horseman went past the open doors. The official led Dave to a teller.

"Forty pound of gold. Twelve thousand dollars," smiled the teller, tying the bag. Dave grabbed the bag from the teller and went out into the street just as a shouting mass of men converged on the bank.

"Hello, Jep," Dave smiled wearily at the familiar figure trying to push nearer the front. Jep stared unbelievingly as Dave handed him the bag of gold. He shook his head slowly.

"How did you do it, kid? Seven hundred miles in six days and nights! You must be made of iron!"

"More like iron that's melting now," Dave said, tottering to stay on his feet. Jep steadied him, then guided him down the street. Then, in a dim room, Jep was easing him down on a bed, swinging his leaden legs up. He heard Jep's voice from far away.

"Dave, do you want to keep them beautiful spurs on?"

"Uh-uh," Dave murmured, smiling sleepily. "I'm not going to be riding any more nightmares . . . not for a long, long while . . ."

Jep's chuckle faded away as Dave sank luxuriously into the deep velvet blackness of sleep.

Stephen Payne

Boss of the Cross-O

"I'll do the best I can, Mr. Farr," Kerry James said, "but I'm scared that horse thief may shoot you, 'stead of you shooting him."

Jack Farr laughed as he stepped down from his saddle to open a gate in a buck-and-pole fence. "Don't worry about that, Button. I'll take care of myself, and until I come back you'll be boss of the Cross-O."

" 'Boss of the Cross-O,' " Kerry repeated soberly, and his gaze roved the ranch. He saw green meadows extending north and south along a willow-lined stream, cattle on a sagebrush bluff beyond the valley, and rugged mountains against the western skyline. Nearer, weathered log buildings and pole corrals, milk cows in one of these enclosures, and a dozen horses pastured nearby.

Weary and footsore, Kerry had arrived in

Jenkins the evening before, and had asked the liveryman if he could work for his supper and sleep in the hayloft. Hod Perkins had given the sturdy, farm-raised boy a probing stare, then had smiled and said, "I reckon."

Later, Kerry confided, "I had chances to work on farms along the trail from Kansas to these Colorado mountains. But I'm dead set on getting to be a real cowboy. Any chance I can get on with an outfit in this cattle country?"

Gravely, Hod had advised, "Take any job you can get, son. Make yourself necessary, and you'll work up to what you want."

Kerry had felt hopelessly discouraged, until this morning, when a rider on a foam-flecked horse had shouted to the liveryman, "Hi! Hod! You know anybody who'll do chores on Cross-O for a day or two?"

"Yep," Hod answered. "Right here's a kid, 'bout seventeen, who savvies chores good 'nuff to please even old Albert Snyder. Jack Farr, meet Kerry James."

Farr had looked no farther. "Come with me, kid," he commanded. "Got a horse?"

Hod answered for the boy. "He can use Club Foot till he comes back to town."

Riding bareback, with only a halter, Kerry had kept pace with Farr's mount while Farr told him several things about the setup on the Cross-O, and then explained, "Albert Snyder and his cowboys are on the calf roundup. I was left at the ranch to do chores. But I've got to chase down a thief who stole a horse last night, and you're to stick on my job."

Now, at the east-line fence of the Cross-O, Farr closed the gate behind Kerry, and rode away at a lope.

Kerry felt just like a triumphant fisherman, even though he'd be doing tiresome jobs with which he was familiar—chores.

After he stalled Club Foot in the big, red-roofed stable, the boy inspected the bunkhouse. Only three of the bunks had bedding. Farr had told him to use one bunk, and allot others to any chance visitor.

Hurrying on to the rambling old main house, Kerry found in a large storeroom both chicken and pig feed, and soon stopped the complaints of the chickens and the pigs. Next, he milked the four cows in the corral, and strained the fresh milk into pans. Before he could feed the hungry calves, however, he had to saw and split wood in order to build a fire in the kitchen range and warm the skim milk.

Eventually, he went to work on the dirty bunk-house, thinking it was great to be boss of a big

cow ranch; gave a fellow such a feeling of re-
sponsibility!

Toward twelve o'clock Kerry heard a horse in
the yard, and stepping out of the now clean bunkhouse, he saw a grizzled, white-haired, stoop-
shouldered man with a sort of forlorn and weary
expression on his lined face. He didn't sit his grey
nag well, and his saddle was old and worn, like
the man himself. But he spoke in a friendly voice.

"Howdy, son. Who're you?"

"I'm Kerry James, sir." Kerry hesitated and
then said, "you look kinda tired, want to rest
awhile here?"

"I am," the stranger answered briefly. "Reckon
I will rest a spell, Kerry. You'll take care of my
horse?"

"Yes, sir. I've heard visitors are always wel-
come on a cow ranch, 'specially if they're kinda
down on their luck."

" 'Down on their luck'?"

"Sure," said Kerry. "I know how it is. I
walked all the way from Kansas, getting hand-
outs—like a tramp. You and me got somethin' in
common, old-timer."

"That so?" the man said. "How come you're
holding down this ranch?"

"I was in Jenkins when Jack Farr came to get
a man to take over this job for him. Jack had to

go after a horse thief. Right now, I'm the boss of the Cross-O."

The man's eyes opened wide; the white and shaggy eyebrows above them lifted high. He gazed intently at the horses in the nearby pasture, and Kerry saw his lips move as if he were counting them.

"Humph!" he said. Then, flinching, as if in pain. "Dog the luck, I'm off my feed. Stomach actin' up." He dismounted and started toward the main house.

"No! Not to the big house!" Kerry cried. "Mr. Snyder and his granddaughter aren't here. But I can't let a range tramp—I mean let anybody— use one of their rooms. Jack Farr said the girl's family lives in town, but she likes to be with her grandfather when he's at home. Mr. Snyder's a widower. She kinder looks after him. . . . You come to the bunkhouse with me."

"I'll bet it ain't your fault you're down and out," said Kerry, and piloted his guest to one of the bunks. "I'll pull off your boots and get a blanket to put over you."

"Thanks, son." The man lay down on the bunk. "You think Farr expected to nail this horse thief?"

"He sure did! Wish I could've gone with him and done somethin' excitin'. I'd hoped to get a

riding job, but I was that desperate I grabbed the chance to work here. I'll do the job right, so it'll suit Mr. Snyder—I hope! . . . What would you like to eat, Pop?"

"Just let me rest for now, Kerry. You're an awful talker."

"Yeah, I guess so." Kerry grinned and went to the house. He was whittling shavings to start a fire when he heard hoofbeats in the yard, stepped to the kitchen door, and had his look at a tall, swarthy fellow in cowboy attire.

The man had dismounted and was glancing around in a somewhat furtive manner, which prompted Kerry's quick thought, "Sly and pretty tough. Maybe he's a horse thief!"

"Hello, mister," he said.

The man stared at Kerry and asked, "Who're you?"

"Kerry James, in full charge of Cross-O."

"That so?" incredulously. "Now who hired a pumpkin-roller like you?"

Anger flared in Kerry. "Don't call me a pumpkin-roller," he snapped. "I'm boss here till Jack Farr comes back, or Mr. Snyder shows up."

"Cool off, kid," the man said, and stepped toward the house. "I know Snyder's with his punchers, on roundup, and I saw Jack Farr in town, so your being here s'prised me."

"Jack Farr's chasin' a horse thief, mister!"

"Chasin' a pair of dice, more likely! Well, I'm here to get my own gear and stuff."

"How come your duffel's here?" asked Kerry sharply.

"That blankety-blanked old Snyder fired me out on the range, and all my stuff was here. So get outa my way, kid."

The fellow's profanity shocked and angered Kerry. "Mr. Snyder ain't what you called him! And you ain't coming in this house. If your duffel's here, it's in the bunkhouse."

A quick glance toward the bunkhouse made Kerry think that for just a moment he glimpsed his elderly visitor's face at the door.

The swarthy man stepped back and clenched his hands. "Pumpkin-roller, you're insinuating I might be a thief!"

"Sure," said Kerry. "Come for your duffel when Mr. Snyder's home. Savvy?"

This, he thought, was the kind of talk a real cowhand would use in the same situation. It produced another burst of profanity, and an angry, "Out of my way, squirt, or I'll whale the daylights out of you."

As if scared, Kerry stepped back and to one side, and reached around for a stick of stovewood. The man was coming through the open door when Kerry's club thudded against his head, and he pitched to the floor.

Instantly, Kerry grasped the man's ankles and coasted him out into the yard and up to his horse, which snorted and turned away. Kerry, however, caught a trailing bridle rein and brought the animal under control.

Swarthy was recovering already, so Kerry plucked the man's six-shooter from its holster and cocked it. "Now you climb on your horse and get. And don't come back till Mr. Snyder's home!" he ordered.

The fellow rolled over, sat up, coughed out a mouthful of dirt, and blinked dazedly. "Don't point that cannon at me! Give it here."

"Nothing doing." Kerry twisted his lips and squinted his eyes, hoping this made him look really tough. "If you ain't gone in ten seconds I'll see how this gun shoots. One—two—three—"

The man leaped on his black, spurred it savagely, and loped out of the yard and away.

Kerry suddenly felt as if his knees would buckle. Hunger forgotten, he went to the bunkhouse and found his earlier guest apparently asleep.

"How you feeling, Pop? Like somethin' to eat now?"

One eye opened. "Feelin' better, son. Feelin' like I had a dose of laughing gas like dentists use. Like I wanted to laugh." And with this he did laugh, whole-heartedly.

This outburst over, he said gravely, "Nothing to eat yet, thanks. That your six-shooter?"

"No. I'm goin' to go put it in Mr. Snyder's room."

He returned to the house, opened cans of corn, pork and beans, and tomatoes for his dinner.

Obviously Jack Farr had been an untidy house-keeper. The kitchen needed a thorough cleaning, and Kerry was hard at this new job when he had a third visitor.

This was a chunky, florid-faced man, wearing plow-shoes and riding a work horse with a blind bridle.

"Where's old man Snyder?" he demanded curtly.

"Mr. Snyder is on a roundup, and I'm—I'm in charge. Something I can do for you?"

The visitor's eyebrows lifted high. "I'm Bill Smith," he said. "Got a homestead over yonder," pointing westward across the wide valley. "Yesterday this doggoned outfit dumped a whaling big bunch of cattle on them flats."

"Mr. Smith," returned Kerry, "this ain't a

doggoned outfit, and it's got a right to dump a herd of cattle wherever it wants to put them."

"How come a squirt like you has the gall to say he's boss of this ranch? Poppycock!" Smith snapped short, work-calloused fingers.

Kerry wanted to be friendly with this farmer, but it seemed as if Smith was deliberately trying to rub him the wrong way. "Jack Farr gave me the job while he's chasing a horse thief," he explained.

"Farr chasing a horse thief!" he said derisively. Then, "Kid, I want old man Snyder to herd them cattle off my claim, and begin doing it right now."

Kerry stared at him. "Your claim's fenced?" he inquired.

"We-ell, no, but—"

"Stop right there, Mr. Smith! To save your grass you can herd cattle off your land. But you haven't got any right to ask this outfit to do it for you."

"Yeah? Well, I'm goin' to open that old hog's fence and run his cattle into his meadow!" Smith turned his heavy-footed horse and rode across the valley.

Kerry gazed after him, badly worried, and somewhat at a loss. Soon, however, he set his lips in a firm line, and turned into the house. When at length he stepped out, a double-barreled shotgun lay against his shoulder.

He was hurrying to the stable when his first visitor put his face out of the bunkhouse. "What's up, Kerry?"

"Aw, some homesteader's on the prod about Cross-O cows eating his grass. He says he's going to turn 'em in our meadow. I'm sayin' he ain't!"

"You be careful with that scatter-gun, son."

"Shucks, it won't kill nothin'. I loaded it with ice cream salt from the storeroom."

The older man's eyebrows were again way up, his mild grey eyes again open very wide. "I see. Want help with this job, Kerry? I might be able to stick on my horse and—"

"You ain't strong enough, Pop, and, not meaning to be disparaging, you wouldn't be any help a-tall. If this deal goes against me and I don't come back, you tell Jack Farr and Mr. Snyder that I did the best I could. S'long."

Kerry led Club Foot out of the barn, and rode across the green meadow toward the buck-and-pole fence on the sagebrush bluff. Here, two or three hundred cattle were crowding the fence, and with a rock Smith was knocking spiked poles loose from the bucks.

"Stop that!" Kerry shouted. "Get on your nag and ride home—pronto!"

Smith pried loose the last pole, opening a full

panel of the fence. "Who'll make me?" he inquired insolently.

The taunt increased Kerry's determination to protect the Cross-O regardless. He attempted to maneuver the shotgun with one hand, but found it impossible while riding bareback and guiding his mount. "You nail those poles back in place," he ordered.

"Brat, I've taken all I'm going to take off you. Git, before I put my rope on you and drag you through the brush."

Smith mounted his horse, and turned to ride around the cattle. But Kerry, using both hands, pulled the shotgun to his shoulder and pressed the trigger.

He saw Smith's horse sort of scrooch up, and leap as if stung by hornets, and he heard Smith yell with pain. In this same instant, however, Club Foot came to life with a terrific snort, and a wild bound tossed Kerry off his back.

Hitting the ground hard, Kerry was momentarily befuddled. When he wiped dirt from his eyes and scrambled to his feet, the cattle were running away. But with a rope in his hands, Smith was sending his horse straight toward him.

Kerry swooped up the shotgun and dodged aside just as Smith's horse all but ran him down. Its rider missed a wild throw with his rope, and as the horse lunged on past Kerry, the boy leveled the shotgun and peppered Smith's back and his mount's rump with his second, and last, charge of salt. With Smith unable to control it, the horse raced crazily around in a short circle, dashed back through the opening in the fence, and fled across the sagebrush plain.

Kerry repaired the fence, caught Club Foot, and rode back to the Cross-O at his horse's best pace.

He found the old man in the yard, evidently waiting for him. "How'd you make out?" he asked curiously.

"I had to show Smith I meant business. But gosh, I feel kinda washed out, though I'd not admit it to a cattleman. I hope Smith don't make no more trouble."

Pop chuckled. "Smith'll keep his trap shut about this incident—and he'll hope you'll do the same. Who was the rider here earlier, and what'd he want?"

"I figure he had a grudge against Mr. Snyder and intended to rob him. There's a little safe in the livin'-room that could be easy opened. You know the fellow?"

An angry spark flashed briefly in Pop's eyes. "Yes—Swart Richley. I . . . I know Snyder fired him because Swart lied about something."

"You take a load off me," said Kerry. "I didn't know if I was right in sending him off. Now, I'm scairt Swart'll come back to get even with me."

"He did come back while you were tangling with Smith." The old man grinned widely. "When he agreed never to show up again, I gave him his gun. Like Smith, he won't be talking about what a kid did to him. So don't worry."

Kerry stared at his guest before he put a new thought into words. "Pop, you're a lot more of a fellow than I allowed. Thanks . . . Well, time to do chores. If you're going to give me a hand by gettin' supper—you really ought to try to earn your board—you can take this scattergun to the house."

The man's expression puzzled Kerry as he said, "Reckon that's right, son."

An hour later, the chores were under Kerry's control, good smells were coming from the kitchen, and he was walking toward the house when a girl rode into the yard.

She was about fifteen, he thought, but she sat her horse as well as any cowboy, and was dressed —well, just the way she should be! Apparently she was surprised to see him, for she said, "Hello!" and then, "Who are you? What are you doing here?"

Kerry couldn't help stammering as he said,

"I'm Kerry James, and Jack Farr hired me to—"

"That good-for-nothing Jack Farr!" she burst out. "I heard he was in town, and I knew he'd be drunk, so I rode out here to do the chores. It looks as if you've milked and everything else. Did you say Jack Farr hired you?"

"Yes," Kerry replied, and after a moment's hesitation, "Did Farr put something over on me?"

"Yes, Kerry. The truth is Jack hated batching alone and wanted to go to town and stay over night. But you don't know who I am, do you? Connie Ford, Albert Snyder's granddaughter."

"Now I get it," Kerry cried delightedly. "Farr told me you often stayed on Cross-O, but not when Mr. Snyder was on a roundup, like he is now. Connie, I've got a visitor maybe you won't like very much. But you'll stay for supper anyhow, won't you?"

The girl dismounted. "I was intending to stay, Kerry, though I was afraid I'd have to do the chores and get my own supper too. You'll stall my horse?"

"Sure," said Kerry. "That's a swell pony, and you have a cowboy saddle, too."

Wistful longing was so apparent in his voice that Connie gave him a searching look before she said, "Who's this visitor you don't think I'll like?

It smells as if he's fixing a bang-up good supper."

"It sure does!" Kerry agreed. "He's a nice fella, but just an old range tramp. He rode in here sort of sick and—"

"Sick?" asked Connie, a startled expression on her pretty tanned face and in her dark blue eyes, as she looked toward the house. Following her gaze, Kerry saw his grubline rider standing by the door.

Turning quickly, the girl faced Kerry, and once again on this eventful day he saw eyebrows lifted above wide-open eyes. "Kerry," she said severely, "that man is my grandfather, Albert Snyder. And you—you—" Abruptly her expression changed, and she began to laugh. "You mistook him for 'an old range tramp.' "

Kerry's legs turned to rubber, the only sound he was conscious of making was like the "oof" of a punctured balloon. Snatching up the bridle reins of Connie's horse, he led it into the stable. But, over his shoulder he saw Connie run to the house and fling herself into her grandfather's open arms.

Kerry led out Club Foot and clambered astride the plug. His world had crashed. Gone his dream of making good on Cross-O.

His heels drummed against Club Foot's ribs. But the horse merely turned around in a circle, and to Kerry's shamed embarrassment, he saw Connie Ford coming on flying feet. "Kerry, where're you going?"

"To hide from you and Mr. Snyder so you'll never see me again. I—I pulled the biggest, most awful boner ever—"

"Don't be silly!" Connie caught Club Foot's halter. "I believe I understand how you feel. But Grandfather says—"

"Here he comes!" Kerry cried, panicked. "Let go the halter rope so I can skin outa here fast."

But "Pop" had arrived, and his wrinkled face was one wide smile. "Son, I've been chuckling till I feel like a new man. You've done me more real good than a doctor."

Laughter stopped him, while Kerry stared in new bewilderment. The ranchman continued: "By jingo, the way you took hold of the work here, and on top of that handled a couple of tough problems, proved that you measure up man-size. Now that this old tramp has earned his board by cooking a good meal, come and eat with us. We won't let Kerry get off the Cross-O, will we, Connie?"

"No," said Connie. Her smile went right into Kerry James. "Grandfather is going to talk to you about a cowboy job."

"Right," said Albert Snyder. "As soon as I can find a choreman to take Jack Farr's place, you'll start wrangling horses, Kerry; and I want to stake you to a good saddle."

Kerry couldn't find his voice, and Connie had to pull him off Club Foot and lead him toward the house.

Between chuckles Albert Snyder asked, "Going to like it here, Shotgun Kid?"

Kerry glanced sideways at Connie. She was even prettier than he'd thought at first. She was the sort of girl a fellow would like—some day—to have for his "steady."

"Going to like it here? Oh, boy! You know it!"

BOYS' LIFE LIBRARY

The Boys' Life Book of Football Stories
The Boys' Life Book of Horse Stories
The Boys' Life Book of Mystery Stories
   Selected by the Editors of Boys' Life
Mutiny in the Time Machine
   by Donald Keith